Thank you

Dark Enough
to See the Stars

Enjoy!

Cindy Noonan

Cindy Noonan

First Edition

Published by
Helping Hands Press

ISBN: 978-1-62208-534-7

Printed in the United States of America

"Trouble is in the land....
But I know, somehow,
that only when it's dark enough
can you see the stars.
And I see God working...."

Dr. Martin Luther King Jr.

Acknowledgements

Many people encouraged and inspired me to write this book. I can't thank them enough for all for their help.

My husband, Frank, and my children, Pam, Kimberly, Chip, Sherri, and Kelly, whose love and support never wavered during the long writing process. I often turned to Kelly for advice, and her wisdom always pushed me forward.

My writers group, Leslee Clapp, Sherry Boykin, Sarah Lynn Phillips, Gail Mills, Jo Ann Walczak, and Becky Loescher, who always believed in me, listened to every chapter, and gave much needed advice about plot, voice, and grammar. They were priceless cheerleaders.

Author Joyce Magnin, whose instruction and editing sharpened my writing and strengthened my story. She suggested I write this book. I never would have attempted an historical novel without her encouragement.

My editor at Helping Hands Press, Marsha Hubler, whose patience and encouragement made the editing process enjoyable.

Finally, I would like to thank Helping Hands Press for their commitment in publishing **Dark Enough to See the Stars**.

Chapter 1
Escape

Mama picked up a corner of her apron and wiped away a tear. Another drop fell, leaving a shiny dark trail on her face. She reached her pillow arms around me and squeezed so tight I couldn't breathe. But I didn't mind. I knew I would never see her again. I let her squeeze me as long as she wanted.

Me and Mama had spent all morning hiking to the train station with all the other slaves from Oakley Plantation. Buck, the overseer, kept prodding us along so's we'd get to the depot for the one o'clock train.

As we walked, Mama took my arm. Her eyes burned like kindling. She had that look she always get when she gonna remind me how I got my name.

She leaned next to me and whispered, "Never forget, Mose, you is named after Moses in the Bible. His mama didn't want him growing up no slave. One day, she just trusted God and floated him down the river. Her child wasn't gonna be a slave no more." She waved her hand like she was pushing baby Moses in that bulrush basket downstream. "And you ain't gonna be one neither. Pretty soon you goin' to the Promised Land. Just like he did."

And now was my chance. If they was gonna rip me away from her like seed outta cotton, then I was gonna be free. We planned for me to make a run for it before she boarded the train. I wanted her to see me get away before that black monster took her. Its long shiny teeth stuck out on the track looking mean and hungry. Somebody called that a cowcatcher. I don't know if it catched any cows, but it was getting ready to swallow Mama and a whole lot of people I knowed all my life.

I poked my toe in the dust by the railroad tracks. The engine puffed steam like a slave driver smoking a cigar. It stung my eyes, but I wasn't gonna cry. I was growed up now—big enough to work the fields. And big enough to run away.

I looked over at my cousins, Zeke and Quin. They used to call me a mama's boy. They wasn't making fun of me now. They was blubbering as much as everybody else.

Masta Bill was selling Mama, but he was keeping me. I could chop wood faster than any darkie on the plantation. He said I was strong as his best mule. I grew so much after harvest last year, I stood a head taller than Mama. So Buck put me to working the tobacco fields this spring. On the first day of planting, Mama reached up and took my big shoulders in her hands. She was proud of how big and strong I got. But she knowed that being strong meant I'd be good in the fields and would never get a chance to be a house slave like her. When she ran her fingers over my back, I knowed she wondered if it would get scarred up rough as hickory bark from the lash.

Buck kept telling all of us who was staying how lucky we was. He carried on about how we get cornmeal and bacon for the week, get to grow vegetables in our own patch, and have a whole week off at Christmas. To hear him talk, you'd think we was gentleman farmers dining on ham and biscuits every Sunday. He probably knows where his mama lives and can visit her whenever he wants. I reckon he ain't got no scars from being whupped neither.

Mama tightened her lips into a smile and slipped a tote over my arm like it was a white man's fine carpetbag. The smoky smell of fatback tickled my nose. She stroked the strap that hung on my shoulder and whispered, "When it gits dark enough, you can see the stars. Remember how I been showin' you, Mose? Look for the Drinkin' Gourd. Don't forgit them two stars at the end of the gourd that point to the North Star. You keep followin' that star."

She sighed and took my big hands in hers like my hands was baby birds. "When you git to the river, follow it till you see a stone house right on the water. That be the mill where they grind the corn. It have a big wheel on its side that turns in the river. The agent said they's waitin' for you. He's a God-fearin' man. I trust him." She shut her eyes and stroked my fingers. She breathed deep and reached for more words. "I know you can do this. The river's gonna save you jus' like it saved Moses. The Lord told me you was free from the day you was born."

I kicked at a weed and tried to keep my eyes on the ground. If I looked in Mama's sorrowful eyes, I'd start bawling.

Her eyes filled up. She let out a wail from deep inside her like earth reaching out to heaven. Nobody noticed. They was all crying, too. Mamas leaving kids. Brothers leaving sisters. All being sold south.

Then she sang me that song. I already knowed it. I heard the folks waiting at the depot sing it over and over like a dove's call, trying to smooth over all them broken hearts.

"When we all meet in heaven, there is no partin' there,

When we all meet in heaven, there is partin' no more."

My heart might of broke if it wasn't for our plans. Mama knowed I was gonna be free. And that made *her* free on the inside.

I heard scuffling. Somebody yelled, "I ain't goin'! I'll die first!"

"Me neither!" another man shouted.

A ruckus broke out. Punches and smacks and groans drowned out the sobbing. Somebody hit Ben, one of Buck's white workers, and knocked him to the ground. Buck drove his horse through the crowd and thrashed a dark body with his whip till he got off Ben.

Mama shook her head. More tears trickled down her face. "That poor soul."

Her eyes lit up. "That fight just gave you the chance you need. Buck's busy settlin' the commotion."

Buck's workers grabbed clubs and beat everybody they could get their hands on. They chained the fighters' arms and legs and threw them in the rail car like they was sacks of corn.

"You gotta leave. Now." She hugged me one last time.

I rushed across the railroad tracks. Snuck behind the train. Stooped under the railroad car and stole one last look at Mama. I saw her backside. She reached behind her to tighten the bow on her apron. Didn't look back, but I swear she waved her hand at me just a little when she let go them apron strings. I slid down the gully and pushed through the brush into the woods.

I bit my fist and stuffed down the wail that wanted to bust out of me. Blinked real hard so the tears wouldn't come. Took a few deep breaths, just like Mama showed me when Buck made us watch him whup Uncle Hank. Back then, Mama had wrapped her arm around me and squeezed me tight.

The tears came anyway. That was better than letting out the scream. I might never feel Mama's pillow arms again.

I ran and ran.

Chapter 2
Through the Woods

I kept away from the road. Out of sight, I could hike a few more miles in daylight—if the briars and sharp rocks didn't slice up my feet.

Didn't wanna look back. That train whistle wailed like folks weeping at a funeral. A whole lotta people I knowed was stuffed inside that coffin headed for hell. Poor Mama.

Don't you worry, Mama. I'm gonna make you proud. You and I have a fine plan. Remember the day Buck told us everybody could go to the train station? I was just happy I could say goodbye and see you off. But you seen a way I could escape. Buck said slaves would run away with no overseer watching over them in the tobacco fields. Figured he and his hands could keep an eye on us better if we all hiked to the depot.

Well, you was wrong, Buck. Dead wrong.

I let myself smile for the first time today.

I heard twigs snap behind me. Somebody was running through the brush. They was after me. Dear God, if they got horses and bloodhounds, I cain't outrun them.

I ran faster. Tripped over a tree root. Fell on my face. I picked myself up. A hand grabbed my shoulder and spun me around. I almost wet my pants.

It was Zeke.

He whispered, "Moses! It's me, Zeke!" His skinny chest heaved from being all out of breath.

My heart pounded like a sledgehammer. "What you doin' here? Does Bitsy know where you are?" I said it louder and sharper than I meant to, but how dare he catch me unawares like that?

"No." He shook his head. Then looked me in the eye. "I'm runnin' away, too."

I looked all around making sure nobody was in earshot. I whispered, "This ain't no place for a child. It's too dangerous." He looked upset, but the last thing I needed was a boy tagging along. Zeke wasn't quite big enough to work in the fields yet. He still was running errands for Miz Oakley. Never done any hard work and never felt the lash. How would he last out here with no food and water?

"Bitsy don't care nothin' 'bout me and Quin. I didn't tell her."

I slapped his arm. "She do, too. She promised yo' mama she'd watch out for you when your mama got sold away."

He looked at me with sorrowful eyes. "Ain't the same, Mose."

For the first time, I knowed how he felt.

I put my arm across his shoulders. "Well, I reckon you can come along. But you gotta do everythin' I tell you."

The sun still hung high in the sky as we snuck through the woods. No stars to point the way in daylight. And no folks we could trust to set us on the right path. Didn't want to walk too far in daylight. Somebody might see us. I wanted to find a hiding place so we could rest up for traveling at night. The sun didn't sink much farther before I spotted one.

A huge rock squatted on the ground like an old toady-frog. Moss covered its back like warts. A huckleberry bush grew right in front of it. I spotted a place behind it big as the cuddy hole where Mama kept turnips.

"I think I found somethin', Zeke. Stay right here while I check it out." I pushed aside branches. They slapped me in the face, but I paid them no mind. I poked in that hole with a stick.

"Don't want no critters keeping us company, 'specially snakes."

I slid behind the bush and sat on the cool ground. The rock leaned out over the top of me like a mama frog on the lookout. Maybe she'd tell me if any slave catchers nearby.

I poked my head out from behind the bush. "Come on."

"No snakes?"

"None I could see."

Zeke crawled in and lay next to me, just like we was in our cabin on the plantation. I always slept on the dirt floor next to him and Quin. But now there was just two of us.

Eight other folks shared that cabin. It got hot as a blacksmith's forge this time of year. Air so thick a body could hardly breathe. In the winter, snow and ice blew right between the house boards.

We lay on the cool ground catching our breath. I nudged him. "Remember the time we snuck the ginger cake Bitsy made for her beau? We ate the whole thing."

Zeke chuckled. "One of the best days of my life. Ooh, she came after us like a mad dog. But the whuppin' we got was worth it. Wished I had some of that ginger cake now." He licked his cracked lips. "What I really want is some water."

I was parched, too. I seen many a body passed out in the tobacco fields working in sun so hot you thought you'd melt. All they needed was a little water.

The huckleberry bush hung right over us. I reached up and picked a few. They was wet and my tongue was dry. "Try these, Zeke." We picked a mess of huckleberries and filled our bellies.

Zeke eyed my tote laying on the ground and picked it up. "What you got in here, Mose?"

I grabbed it from him. "Now just hold on." I twisted the cord of my tote around my finger. Mama had filled it with two ashcakes and a slice of fatback. I aimed to eat some today and save the rest for tomorrow. Hadn't made no plans to share. Having Zeke along changed everything. I loosed up the cord and peeked in my sack. I handed him an ashcake. "Here. We'll eat the fatback tomorrow."

I stuffed the ashcake in my mouth, scratched up some fallen leaves, and lay on the damp dirt. "Try to rest up for now. We got a lot of walkin' to do tonight."

I hugged my tote. It smelled like Mama. She spent her nighttimes sewing it out of the tow linen shirt I wore last year. She done a fine job, doubling the cloth for strength and putting in a drawstring. Strong enough to hold anything I wanted. I hoped it would hold a whittling knife someday.

Miz Oakley always told my mama what fine party gowns she sewed for her. Missus cried and carried on when Master Bill let her know he was selling Mama. We heard them squabbling about it all the way to the slave quarters. Didn't make sense he would get rid of one of Missus' favorites. Somebody musta told lies about her. Come to think of it, I saw Simon, the blacksmith, wearing a new felt hat the other day. I bet it was him. He told on Lettie last winter when she stole a chicken when everybody was hungry. He showed off a fancy new pipe to smoke after that. Everybody watch him now and tell him nothing.

I decided I better quit scaring myself thinking about bad stuff. I closed my eyes and smiled. Mama woulda liked my hidey-hole. I know what she'd say. "Why the Lord hisself make that for you. He knowed you need it today. That a house right from heaven."

Chapter 3
Danger

I woke up when Zeke jabbed me with his elbow. He was still asleep. That boy never could lie still. I hoped he wasn't gonna be no trouble. Could he keep up with me?

I crawled out from under the rock and looked at the black sky poking through the treetops. The moon shone bright and round and full. Moonlight made it easier to see where we was going. And stars! Lots of stars winking at me.

I snuck up to a clearing so I could see better. Them stars looked like a lot of tobacco blossoms pinched off and scattered every which way across the sky. I grinned when I found the Drinking Gourd. The four stars that made up the cup and the three stars that made the handle grinned back.

Mama showed me how to spot the Drinking Gourd many times. She'd point to it, have me close my eyes, spin around, and look up. "Okay, Mose. Find it yousself now," she'd say, until I got to know where it was every time.

I asked her one day, "How come you so smart about that star? I never hear Gramma tell about it." She grinned real big like a barn cat dragging home a bird. Then looked around and made sure nobody could hear. "Remember that tinker who come to fix the kitchen pots? He a conductor for the Underground Railroad."

"The wha-a?"

She put her hand over my mouth and shushed me good. "Not a real railroad," she whispered. "It be folks who help slaves get free."

"How they do that?"

"They tell folks where to run, and show 'em houses to hide at where they be safe until they get north. Stuff like that." She put both hands on her hips and looked up in the night sky. "The tinker told me about it."

She pointed to the stars at the end of the Drinking Gourd. "Don't forget, them two stars help you find it. They's like God's little finger pointin' to the North Star. He put that star there for folks like us, so's we could find our way. He knowed when he made the world there'd be lost folks who needed to git home."

"Yes'm," I said. I always wished for the day I could follow that star.

Now it was here.

I crawled back into our hidey-hole and stuck a toe in Zeke's ribs.

"Yaaah!" He grabbed my foot.

I slapped a hand over his mouth and whispered, "Zeke. It's me, Moses. You with me now. Gotta keep quiet. You coulda been heard across three counties. Never know how close them slave catchers might be."

He gasped and blubbered. "I'm sorry, Mose. I…I'll be quiet. Promise. Jus' don't scare me like that next time."

"Okay." Had to remember he was still a child. I grabbed his hand and pulled him up. "We gotta get goin'."

"Mose, how we know where to go?"

I put an arm around him and pointed at the sky. "There's a special star up there called the North Star. We gonna follow that star. Just step lightly. We don't wanna step on no critters."

I didn't let on I was worried about snakes. In daylight I could watch the ground, but in the dark I never knowed what crawled under my feet. A snakebite could kill us in a few days if the wolves didn't get us first.

Zeke grabbed my arm. "Mose. I hear somethin'."

We stopped.

A man shouted. Sounded like somebody was yelling at a mule. Maybe a farm nearby.

I heard whines, yelps…barking.

That wasn't no mule.

Dogs.

My heart raced like a runaway horse, but my legs felt like trees stuck in the ground.

Zeke's eyes grew wide. He started to yell.

I clapped a hand over his mouth. "Hush up." I yanked on his arm and we ran. We pushed through brush, leaped over logs, ducked around trees.

I tripped and fell. Sliced my hand on a rock. Blood gushed out. I pressed my hands together to stop the bleeding. I could hear them dogs getting closer.

It was bad enough I was gonna get caught. I could take the whupping. But now they was gonna get Zeke, too. Didn't seem right.

Zeke knelt down next to me. He whispered, "Mose...you okay?"

I looked him in the eye. "Listen to me real good, Zeke. Remember when I told you you gotta do everythin' I say?"

He nodded.

"Well, them slave catchers are too fast for us. They's gonna be on us any time now."

He curled himself up and started crying.

I poked him with my elbow. "Look at me and listen. This is real important.... Ain't no reason they need to get us both."

His eyes got big as a scared rabbit. "Whatchu mean?"

"I mean I'm gonna let them see me. When they do, they'll come after me. You hightail it the other away."

He started bawling again. "I cain't let them get you, Mose. Besides, where would I go?"

"Go home."

"But they'll whup me good. And I don't know how to get there."

"You're a child, and Miz Oakley won't let Buck beat you like he will me. Tell 'em you wandered off looking for berries and got lost. If you go back the way we came, you'll find the depot. Just follow that road, and it'll take you home. Goin' back on your own is better'n gettin' caught runnin' away."

The dogs howled louder and louder. They sounded hungry. A slave catcher shouted, "The dogs are on to him, Sam."

"Get ready to run, Zeke."

He grabbed my arm. "I'll never forget what you done for me, Mose. I won't tell on you, neither." Zeke took off fast as those skinny legs could carry him.

I stood up, hoping they could see me in that moonlight.

"There he is! Sic him, Bandit! Get him, Lobo! Don't let him get away."

I began running in front of them dogs, drawing them away from Zeke. I kept pushing myself on, even though there wasn't no breath left in me. Had to give Zeke as big a lead as he could get.

Wasn't long before I got dizzy. Trees looked like they was spinning around me. My knees gave way. I fell on the ground and started crawling. My hand touched something hard. A fallen log. I pushed aside the brush around it and crawled under. I lay still and waited for them bloodhounds to rip me apart.

Twigs kept snapping as the slave catchers pushed closer. Them devil dogs barked louder and louder.

Suddenly, them barks turned into whines.

"Yeeow! A skunk. Jehosaphat! The dogs are gonna lose the scent."

Something big leaped over my log. Way too big for a skunk.

Them dogs. No. Cain't be. I heard them yowling behind me like they been stung by a nest of bees. Musta been a deer.

A pair of black boots stomped by, leading a horse. It reared. Almost stepped on me. "Easy, girl," the man in boots said.

Another man said, "Tarnation. These dogs been ruined for the search. Lobo, come on."

They chased the deer.

I figured any time now they would turn around and find me. Yank me out of my hiding place. Them hounds kept whining. Them slave catchers kept griping. Finally I couldn't hear them no more. They was gone.

Thank you, God, for the skunk.

Thank you, God, for the deer.

Thank you, Mama, for your prayers.

I looked at my hand. The bleeding had stopped. I shut my eyes and fell asleep.

Chapter 4
The Mill

Something tickled my arm. I opened my eyes. Flicked a beetle off my skin. Where was I? My head ached like Buck been kicking it with his black boot.

Black boots.

Bad dream. But it wasn't a dream. I thought about them slave catchers and started to shiver. But then I had to smile. I smelled like skunk. Felt like plantation lady perfume to me.

Didn't know how long I been sleeping, but it was daylight. I crawled out from under my log. My heart pounded. I wanted to run. How long would it take for them hounds to figure out they was on the wrong trail? When would they come after me?

I tiptoed through the brush, hating the scritchy-scratchy sound my feet made. If I made any noise, I'd be dog meat. Didn't hear no slavers. Heard birds singing instead. Was they warning me about them devil dogs?

I hoped Zeke found his way back. More than anything, I didn't want them slave catchers to find him.

No. I was sure they was still after me.

Had to keep walking. Wasn't gonna look for no hidey-hole today. If I didn't find the river, the dogs could be on me once they lost the smell of that skunk.

Never seen a river before. I asked Mama what one look like, and she said it bigger than a creek. She said you cain't wade across it and be careful. Don't get out above your head or the river will have you for dinner.

I pushed through the woods. Listened for dogs. Sniffed for wood smoke. Didn't want to walk right into the slaver's camp.

Something smelled different. Not smoke. Not pine. Not dirt. It smelled wet. The ground felt cool. I wrapped my arm around a tree trunk and looked between the trees.

The river.

I waded in, dunked my head, and took a big drink. I wanted to splash and holler, but didn't dare make no noise.

River didn't jabber like no creek. Moved slow and quiet like it was used to keeping secrets. I waded next to the bank. Didn't get in too deep like Mama said.

Had to watch my step on the slippery rocks but I was smiling for the first time today. Them bloodhounds couldn't smell me in the water. The river was saving me, just like Mama said.

I squinted and looked upriver, trying to see the mill. Sure hoped it wasn't the one the plantation used. Many a time I helped Uncle Hank load burlap bags of corn on the wagon. That corn came back from the mill ground up into flour in fine cotton sacks.

What did a mill look like anyway? Mama said the mill looked smaller than the Big House, and the wheel stood half as tall as the mill.

Something slithered against my leg. I jumped almost clean out of the water. Hoped it wasn't a water snake. Maybe it was a frog. I kept wading.

The river made a turn through the woods in front of me. I heard water splashing. Made me stop in my tracks. Hoped slave catchers and dogs hadn't spotted me.

I rounded the bend. A stone's throw away, a big wheel fixed to the side of a house turned in the water. Hollowed out boxes like drinking gourds scooped up the water, rode to the top of the wheel, and dumped water back in the river on the ride down. If that giant wheel was thirsty it wasn't getting much.

I looked for a place to climb out of the water. A tree limb hung over the river like a hand waiting for me. I pulled myself onto the bank and lay flat on the dry ground. No more worrying about slipping on rocks and going under. Mama would be proud I made it this far. This river wasn't gonna have me for lunch.

I scratched my leg. Felt a slimy blob.

Lordy. A fat, black leech sucked on my ankle. *It* was having me for lunch. All this time I thought a snake brushed by me.

I pulled it. It wouldn't budge. Then I remembered what Uncle Hank told us when Bitsy's boy got a leech wading in the creek.

"Push you thumb against you skin next to that sucker mouth. It'll listen to you thumb an' let go."

I did like Uncle Hank said. I threw that sucker back in the water.

A twig snapped behind me. Something or somebody was sneaking up on me. I thought about them bloodhounds licking their chops. I leaped to my feet and turned around.

I yelped and jumped backwards. Didn't mean to, but I was so expecting a slaver to come up on me, I couldn't help myself.

A black boy a little taller than me stood in front of me. He had meat on his bones, like he got plenty to eat. He wore a fine cotton shirt like white folks. Wasn't no tow linen like what Master gave us every year. Most surprising, he wore shoes. In the middle of summer, mind you.

He grinned real big, like he was expecting me, and held out his hand. "Hi, I'm Joel."

My mouth hung open like a barn gate. I looked down at myself. There was blood all over my shirt, and I smelled like skunk. And he wanted to shake my hand.

Never had nobody shake my hand when I'm all cleaned up, let alone when I smelled like a dog that's been picking through trash. I wiped my hands on my pants. My pants was wet. So was my tote. I shook his hand anyway.

He looked me in the eye. "You, by any chance, be Moses?"

I nodded slowly.

"Agent in Frederick told us to expect you." He pinched his nose with his fingers. "Hoo-eee. Looks like trouble found you. We better get you a bath and some clothes. I been prayin' you'd make it."

I smiled. "Nobody been prayin' more than my mama."

He laughed. "I got a prayin' mama, too." He slapped an arm around my shoulder. "Let's get up to the mill before anybody sees us."

Chapter 5
A Place to Hide

I followed Joel up the dirt path that led to the mill. A thick iron bolt, big as a wood plank, locked the mill door. Joel slid it back. It shushed, like it was hushing everybody. We hurried in. Joel shut the door.

"My mama worries about me helpin' slaves," he whispered. His eyes darted back and forth like he was looking out for any trouble. "Come on."

Corn flour covered the floor like frost. Just smelling it made my mouth water.

We walked by two of the biggest rocks I ever seen. My jaw about dropped to my knees.

Them rocks looked like big wheels laying flat on their sides, one on top of the other. They was all joined together with pipes and gears to a big piece of metal, hitched together like two horses to a wagon.

"Ever been in a mill before?"

I shook my head.

He pointed to the big metal funnel at the top. "That's the hopper. You pour corn in up there. It runs down between the two stones. Turns into flour."

He pressed his lips together. "I wonder where Miller Johnson's gonna put you. Can't stay at the house. A couple of families are ridin' in tomorrow with wagonloads of corn. Folks usually make a day of it and catch up on the news." He rubbed his chin and looked me in the eye. "It's important you do exactly what I tell you—and don't go wanderin' around. I'm gonna fetch you some clothes, and a bucket of water so you can scrub up. Wait here till I come get you."

He walked out and locked the door. My belly knotted up. I stared at them two big stones. They wasn't horses hitched together. They was two big lips smacking. And I was their next meal.

I spotted some flour sacks somebody'd throwed in a corner. I lay on the floor and covered myself in case somebody besides Joel came in. The burlap tickled my nose. Made me wanna sneeze. I tried to hold my breath.

The door creaked open. Feet clomped toward me.... I took a peek. Big black boots.

That ain't Joel.

A hand reached down and yanked the sack off me.

I throwed my arms over my head and waited for the blows.

A hand grabbed my arm and pulled me up to my feet. A large white man with leathery skin and a white beard stared at me. His face stretched into a smile. He let go my arm. "Fret thee not, son. I am Miller Johnson. Glad to know thee."

My heart pounded. I tried to breathe but couldn't get no air. When I caught my breath, I answered him respectful-like. "Thank you, sir."

He handed me a rag and a bar of soap. "Joel mentioned ye might need a bath." A bucket of water sat on the floor. He stirred it with his finger. "Good and warm." He set a shirt and pair of pants next to the bucket. "When ye have washed and dressed, let's get thee over to the house. My wife is cooking dinner. After we eat, I will put thee up in the barn. It's safer there." He walked out of the mill.

Joel came in to fetch me after I cleaned up. He nodded and smiled. "Not bad, not bad. My shirt and pants from last year fit you mighty fine."

"Thank you for lettin' me borrow your clothes."

"Well, they's yours now. Don't fit me anymore."

I ran my hand down the shiny smooth buttons. Now I had me a fine white shirt. I wasn't dressed like a slave no more.

Joel threw his arm around my shoulder and we walked up to the house.

Miller Johnson's place wasn't as grand and fancy as the Big House on Oakley Plantation but was a lot nicer than the slave quarters. It was made of fine, thick logs. All the gaps was plastered with mud and whitewashed, giving the house a lot of nice looking stripes. A split rail fence surrounded the place. Black-eyed Susans bloomed next to the door and three chickens scratched around the yard. Beans, squash, and the like grew to overflowing in a truck patch next to the house. Behind the garden stood a smokehouse and some outbuildings. A couple of hitching posts stood next to the barn.

Inside, Miz Johnson hunkered over a wood-fire stove, turning fish in a iron skillet. She tucked a loose bit of gray hair back into her bun and wiped her hands on her apron. Her plain brown dress wasn't near as fine as the fancy dresses Master's wife, Miz Oakley, wore. But Miz Johnson's smile made all the fretting I been doing melt like fresh churned butter.

"Welcome, Moses," she said.

Joel came in toting a load of wood and set it down next to the stove. Miz Johnson opened the stove door. "Ye brought that wood at a good time, Joel. Perhaps ye could stoke this fire."

"'Yes'm." He set another log on the fire and then went about setting forks and tin plates on a big wood table in the middle of the room.

I ain't never held a fork before. Never set a table, neither. I didn't wanna be in nobody's way, so I stood by the spinning wheel next to the stairs that went up to the sleeping place. I expected they would let me and Joel eat when they got done. Maybe they'd even let me use a fork. If I watched Mr. Miller eat with his fork, I knew I could learn how to use one proper.

Miz Johnson waved me over as she dished out fish and grits. "Come sit thee down, Moses."

I raised my eyebrows. "Pardon me, ma'am?" I looked at the ground. Forgot I shouldn't look white folks in the eye. I'd be lucky to get any vittles now.

"Well, don't just stand there. Sit thee down."

"Beggin' your pardon, ma'am, but where do y'all want me to sit?"

She cocked her head. "Why, at the table, young man." She took my hand and led me to a chair.

My mouth hung open. Any minute now Mama would tell me to shut it or I'd catch some flies. Never dreamed I'd sit at a fine table with white folks. Joel pulled out a chair across from me and the Johnsons sat on either end.

Miller Johnson bowed his head. "We thank thee, Lord, for thy great bounty and for our new friend. Amen." We all looked up. Miller Johnson looked me right in the eye.

That sent a chill crawling up my back. Brought back to mind when I saw Masta Bill smack Bitsy upside the head when she gave him the eye. He told her she impudent. Never heard that word before, but figured it amounted to sass. And here this white man's looking right at me and calling me a friend.

Miller Johnson passed me the platter. I stuck a crispy brown fish with my fork, just like he did, and plopped it on my plate. Made my mouth water.

I watched Miller Johnson, careful-like, as he cut his fish into little pieces with his fork. He stabbed one and popped it in his mouth. I cut mine just like he did and took a bite. Melted in my mouth like Christmas chicken. My belly was smiling now. I got the hang of using a fork right fast.

Joel and I washed the dishes. He peeked out the door to make sure nobody was coming up the road and then walked me out to the barn.

A chestnut horse with a star on his forehead snorted at us from his stall. Joel rubbed his nose. "That's his way of sayin' hello. Meet Starlight."

"How do, Starlight." I patted his forehead and looked him in the eye. Looking a horse in the eye was easy.

Barn cats meowed behind us. Joel pointed to a hay cart in the corner. "Take a look under that wagon." A calico cat jumped out of a box and bee-lined toward Joel. He scooped her up and held her toward me. I scratched her behind her ears, but she wasn't taking to me. "She's lookin' for cream, but she's got to wait for milkin' time," he said. He put her back in the box.

Chapter 6
A Writing Stick

I woke in a sweat. Sat upright. Bolted out of my bed and almost tumbled over the edge.

Had a dream so real I felt them dogs breathing down my neck. I wiped sweat off my forehead.

I closed my eyes and sank back down on my bed. I tried not to think about what might happen later. It was bad enough my dreams kept reminding me.

"Hullo, Mose. How you doin' up there?"

I looked over the edge.

Joel stood below me, grinning, with a pail in his hand. "Sleep okay?"

I smiled back. "Best night since I left home."

He climbed a couple rungs and handed up the bucket. "Here comes breakfast."

I pulled the pail into the loft and sniffed butter and biscuits. Sweet heaven.

The milk cow started mooing, reminding Joel it was milking time. "I'll be back." He hopped down the ladder and walked out to the pasture.

I peeked out the hayloft window. Rooster already woke up Sun. Now Sun stretched his fingers up to Sky, trying to wake him up, too.

I lifted the napkin out of the bucket and unfolded it. Sure enough, buttered biscuits, just like my nose told me, and a hardboiled egg besides. Ain't had an egg since Mama snuck one from the Big House.

Joel walked in the barn. He led the milk cow to the hitching post and tied her up so's she wouldn't kick over the milk pail. "Come on down and stretch your legs while I milk Missy May. Ain't expecting folks till almost noon."

Missy May's udder was so full it looked tight as a pig bladder balloon. Joel sat on the milk stool, wiped down Missy May's teats and started pulling them in a regular motion. The first squirts hit the pail with a swoosh. Wasn't long before the bucket was foaming with milk white as a cloud. Missy May mooed soft like she felt a whole lot better.

The cats ran up to Joel, rubbing against his legs like flies on sugar. He poured some milk in Mama Cat's bowl. "Here, Patches." He set her dish down in a corner and all them kittens jumped at it too.

I climbed down the ladder. Maybe now was a good time to talk to Joel. My head been filling up with questions like a creek full over its bank. Didn't know where to start.

I squatted next to him. "Can I ask you somethin'?"

He peeked at me over his shoulder. "Like what?"

I picked up a piece of hay and rolled it between my fingers. "Well, like...do you got papers?"

"You mean—am I a free man?" He grinned without taking his eyes off of the pail. "I guess I'm lucky. I was born free."

"You mean your papa was free?"

"Yep. My pappy saved his master's life. So he set him free."

"How he do that?"

"One day Pappy drove his master into town with a load of tobacco. As they were riding down the road, a robber held them up at gunpoint. My Pap swung off the wagon and kicked the gun right out of the man's hand. Pappy took a bullet in his leg. His master was so grateful, he started paying him for the work he did."

Joel wiped off Missy May's teats again and moved the pail of milk out of her way. He led her back to the pasture.

Now I know my mama woulda said it ain't none of my business, but I was itching to know if Joel lived with the Johnsons. When he came back I asked him.

He grinned big and didn't seem atall put out. "I work for Miller Johnson during the week and walk home on Friday before it gets dark. I live a couple miles away."

"If'n you don't mind my askin'...he pay you money?"

"Well, what I get goes to my pa. When I'm twenty-one, I get to keep what I earn. That's the law. But Miller Johnson gives me something a whole lot better than money. Here, let me show you."

He cleared straw from a patch of the barn floor, threw a handful of dirt on it and smoothed it out. For the likes of me, I couldn't figure out how dirt could be better'n money. Then he picked up a twig and snapped it the size of a string bean. But what he did next had me scratching my head. He knelt down and marked with it in the dirt.

"See? I can write my name. J-O-E-L. I'm learnin' to read and cipher, too. My pappy says because Miller Johnson is teachin' me, I'll be able to work a good job and not be stuck plowin' and plantin' for somebody else all my life."

My eyes musta growed big as those biscuits I had for breakfast. Lord in heaven, I ain't never knowed a black man who could read and write. Master always said if you showed a darkie how to read, you just opened a barn gate and let all the cows wander. Teach a slave to read and he'd run off in no time.

"Remember when Miller Johnson came in the barn last night? He was fetchin' me for my lesson."

"But ain't there white folks gettin' mad at you for book learnin'?"

He snorted. Wiped his name out of the dirt. "Well, I don't let just anybody know. Especially folks like Mr. and Mrs. Morgan. He spit out that name like it was a cuss word. "They'll be here in about an hour. Folks like them don't think even free blacks should get educated." But then his frown melted away and his eyes twinkled like he had a big secret. "Mose?"

"Yeah?"

"You wanna learn to write your name?"

I sucked in my breath. "Couldn't that get you in a heap of trouble?"

His eyes sparkled some more, like North Star showing the way. "That's the kind of trouble I like. Since Miller Johnson has me reading the Bible, I even know how to spell your name. It starts with an 'M.' He smoothed out the dirt again. Then he drew some lines that looked like two mountains and handed me the stick. "Here. You try it."

Last time I drew a line in the dirt I was playing tug o' war with Zeke, Quin, and the other boys. But this wasn't no play. I was commencing to learn a most magical thing. Write my name same as Masta Bill do. I held that stick like it was a fine feather quill. I scratched four lines and made them look like two mountains.

Joel smiled. "Hey, you learn quick. The next letter is an 'O'."

He drew a big circle like a wheel. That was easy. The next letter, "S," looked like a snake. My name had two of them. In between the two snakes was "E." It looked like a ladder with one side missing.

Joel clapped me on the back. "You did it!"

I stared at them scratches I made. Mountains. A wheel. And snakes with Jacob's ladder right in between.

I couldn't get no words out. My mouth just didn't work. Yesterday I got to hear a white man say my name proper and call me friend. Today I got to see what my name look like and write it, too. I handed Joel the stick.

He pushed it back to me. "Put the stick in your bag so you can practice whenever you want."

I nodded. Hoped he knowed how grateful I was.

"I better leave before folks start comin'." He dipped me out some milk in a tin cup then picked up the pail and walked back to the house.

I climbed into the loft and sipped the warm milk. How I wished Mama could see me now. Eating fine food and learning my name. She'd be so proud.

I put the stick in my bag. I had something special to keep in my tote now. I had me a writing stick.

Chapter 7
Company

Joel finished up my lesson none too soon. Wagons rumbled and horses clip-clopped. Folks was coming up the road. My belly knotted up. I pulled the ladder up into the loft.

I scooted against the wall and scooped hay all over me till just my head poked out. I knowed them slave catchers could jump me any time. I could be hog-tied and drug back to the plantation by the end of the day. Would Masta Bill offer a reward for bringing me in? What would I fetch? Fifty dollars? I bet the Morgans could use fifty dollars.

The rumbling stopped. Horses snorted. Miller Johnson talked to a man about his load of corn. A woman's voice drifted through the air like butter on grits. "Be careful down by the river, you hear?" The kids chattered like birds.

Another wagon came up the road. "Whoa, easy girl." A new set of horses stopped. Folks hardly had time to say their hellos when a woman's voice screamed like a train whistle, slicing right through the peace and quiet. "I'll tan your hide, Daniel, if you get into any trouble."

A boy drawled slow as molasses, "Y-e-s, ma'am." Sounded like sass to me.

"And mind your little sister," the woman ordered.

Miller Johnson and another man talked. I heard Joel, too. "Yes sir. Right away, sir. I'll get them sacks off the wagon for you."

The barn door creaked opened. Footsteps. I crawled as far into my corner as I could.

A young 'un's voice squealed right under me. Gave me the cold shivers. I swallowed hard.

Two women folk stopped jabbering out front. One of them yelled, "Daniel, go check on your sister. She's in the barn."

He whined. "But I wanna go down to the river."

"You see if she's all right *first*, Daniel Morgan."

Morgan? I closed my eyes and prayed. I heard Daniel and his sister laughing and romping in the hay.

"Ooh, Danny. I hear kittens. Let's go find them."

"Who cares? I wanna go to the river."

"Here they are! Aren't they cute? Ooh, I want this little striped one," his sister said.

Danny cackled in a mean way.

A kitten screeched.

"Hey, let go my kitty," the girl said. "I found her first. Get your own kitten, Danny. Stop it. This one's mine. There's three others to pick from."

"Fine."

Mama cat hissed like she was cornered.

Danny yelped. "Why you worthless fur ball. I'm gonna get you! Look, Clara. She scratched me all the way down my arm."

I heard a soft thud. Mama cat let out a choking cry.

"No, Danny. Don't kick her again," Clara sobbed.

Clara ran out of the barn shouting. "Mama, Mama! Don't let Danny kill the cat. She has babies."

I peeked one eye out the window. Clara hugged her mama's skirt and pulled her toward the barn.

I squatted back down and hid in the hay.

Danny's mom and her train whistle voice stood right under me. "Daniel Morgan, you leave them cats be."

"She scratched me, Mama. Look what she done to my arm."

"Just be glad she didn't scratch your eyes out. You shoulda left them cats alone, 'stead of stirrin' up trouble."

"Clara picked one up first."

"Well, you're big enough to know better."

"What's the fuss in here?" a man's voice barked.

"Daniel is—" Clara said.

"Hush up, child. Daniel, you leave them barn cats alone. We got cats enough at home."

"Yessir." His voice sounded lowly, like a black boy answering his master.

"And no fishin' in the river for you."

"But Pa—"

"You heard me. I need help toting sacks. Come on."

All the jabbering floated outside. I took a couple of deep breaths and laid there, eyes wide open. A little bird hopped onto the loft window and tilted his head at me, like a friend. I know what he saying. "What you worried about child? If God take care of me, he sho' 'nuff can take care of you."

I closed my eyes and fell asleep.

Chapter 8
The Argument

Yelling woke me up. Sounded like Daniel's dad.

"He's free? So what? That boy ain't got no right to be reading. Ain't right for darkies to be showing up whites, makin' 'em look like fools. That's uppity as all get-out. Land sakes, what is happenin' in this world when there ain't no respect for white folk."

I peeked out the window. Miller Johnson was helping Mr. Morgan load sacks of flour onto his wagon. Mr. Morgan's back was to me and he was so busy hollering at the miller I figured I could risk looking out the window some more.

Miller Johnson's eyes squinted like my mama's when she about ready to whup me for something. His ears got red. I could tell he was holding his words back.

Mr. Morgan pulled a blue bandanna out of his pocket and wiped his face. His cheeks bulged with a plug of chaw.

Miller Johnson tossed the last sack in the wagon and straightened up. He stuck his thumbs in his suspenders and spoke all gentle-like, but his eyes was shooting bullets. "Mr. Morgan, are ye telling me ye hast never learned to read?"

Mr. Morgan sputtered. Coughed.

Miller Johnson let go of his suspenders. His eyes softened. "Because if that be so, I would be happy to teach thee."

Mr. Morgan spit slimy black tobacco on the ground, just missing the miller's shoe. "That ain't got nothin' to do with it." He pulled himself onto the buckboard. "Martha!" She looked up from talking to Mrs. Johnson and the other lady. "Call the kids and tell 'em it's time to go."

Mrs. Morgan picked up her skirt and hustled down to the river, tooting, "Wagon's loaded. Daniel, go get Clara."

Daniel ran down to the riverbank. "We gotta go, Clara." He came back pulling his sister in tow.

"Ow! You're squeezin' my hand, Daniel." He didn't let go till they both reached the wagon. They scrambled on top of the flour sacks like fleas on a hound.

As his wife climbed in the wagon, I swear, Mr. Morgan gave the miller the evil eye. "You better watch yourself, Mr. Johnson. Not everybody will do business with nigguh-lovers." He snapped the reins and rumbled off. The wagon wheels kicked up dust like the devil himself was leaving.

I watched to see if Mr. Morgan put a spell on Miller Johnson. But the miller didn't look scared at all. I reckon all them angels around him kept him from that evil eye. He just smiled and stood there with his arms folded, calm as a duck on a pond. He showed that bully what for without lifting a finger.

Joel and the miller commenced loading the other wagon. The butter on grits voice called her kids. "Almost time to go. Hurry up, now."

I hunkered back down in the hay. When the jabbering outside stopped and the wagon rumbled away, I knowed everybody was gone.

Didn't want no more excitement for the day. Just thinking about them words Mr. Morgan said sent a shiver up my back. Made me think of Buck, the overseer. He always called us nigguhs. But I knowed better. That wasn't my name. And I wasn't gonna let no dirty name stick to me no more.

I pulled my writing stick out of my tote and tried to scratch my name on the loft floor. I pressed real hard, but my stick was too soft. I found a small, pointy rock in the corner and scratched with that. M-O-S-E-S. I rubbed my fingers over the letters. They couldn't be wiped away like dirt.

My name was Moses. My mama gave me that name. And a white man said it like it was special.

Maybe another runaway would learn his name special too. Maybe he write his name next to mine. Maybe a whole lotta folks scratch their names here someday, and each one say, "I am somebody, and I am free."

I laid back on my tick and closed my eyes.

Before long, the barn door opened. "Hullo up there."

I leaned over. Joel grinned, holding a bowl of rabbit stew. "Here's your supper. Mr. Johnson thought it'd be safer for you to eat up here, just in case we get more company."

I took a whiff. "Lordy. Is that what I been smellin' cookin' all day? No wonder my belly's been growlin'."

Joel handed it up to me, then climbed up and sat down cross-legged. He cracked his knuckles and made a face like the stew he ate didn't set so well. But I figured it wasn't the stew churning his innards.

"You think Mr. Morgan will make trouble?" I asked.

He shrugged. "Hard to say."

"How'd he find out? Nobody knowed the miller was teachin' you, did they?"

He stretched his legs out and leaned on his elbow. "I always tuck my school books in my bedroll and stash it behind the spinning wheel. Clara must have been snoopin' around. Why she rolled out my bed, I don't know. But she brought my reader outside, waved it at her mama, and said she wanted to play school." He shook his head. "Now everybody in the county will know the miller's teachin' me." He stared out the window with that same look he had when he telling me all men should be free. Looking at the sky like he wanted to fly the coop.

He picked up the pointy rock I been writing with, slammed it against the wall, and watched it bounce on the loft floor. Wouldn't you know, that rock landed right next to my name. One corner of his mouth turned up. The twinkle in his eye came back. "Nice job, Mose."

I picked up my pointy rock and handed it to him. "Hey…write your name next to mine."

He grinned wide and carved each letter slow and careful.

"Hoo-wee. Nice job, Joel. When I can read and write, I gonna tell everybody—got my first learnin' from Joel. He showed me how to write my name."

He tossed the rock up against the wall again, but this time he laughed. "You gonna make me famous, eh?" He stepped down the ladder a few rungs and leaned his elbows on the loft floor. "Tomorrow is the big day, Mose."

I sucked in my breath. "Yeah, I'm countin' on them angels comin' by to help me out." I said it with a grin. Didn't want to let on I was scared.

He smiled. "Don't worry. You'll be snug as a bug hidin' under that false bottom. Like I said before, Miller Johnson ain't lost nobody yet." He climbed down the ladder. "I got to get home before dark. Ain't seen Ma and Pappy all week." He waved good-bye.

I lay back down on my straw tick and took a deep breath. What did a false bottom look like? Would he lay me under all them sacks of corn flour? What if I couldn't breathe? Just thinking about it riled my stomach again.

But I had to remember that every day God brought me to a safe hidey-hole. I had to believe he'd bring me to another one tomorrow.

Chapter 9
The Wagon

I was already awake when Miller Johnson walked in the barn. "Moses."

I peeked over the edge of the loft. He smiled at me like he just busting to show me something. "Come on down. I believe it is safe for thee to eat with us this morning."

I grabbed my tote and scrambled down the ladder, glad to walk around a spell. I stopped at the barn door. Stretched my legs like a cat waking up from a nap. My arms and legs been taking it easy a long time. I told them they got to get strong because this trip ain't over yet.

I poked my head out the barn door and looked down the road. Couldn't see no wagons. Couldn't hear no drivers yelling giddy up, neither. I took a deep breath. Bacon. I liked that smell a heap better than the hay and horse manure I been sniffing for the last two days. Me and Miller Johnson moseyed on up to the house.

Five flapjacks and all the bacon I could eat filled my belly. Mrs. Johnson kept passing me more bacon. Didn't want to disappoint her none by turning it down.

"A strapping young man needs to eat," she said.

A yellow hound hung around the table waiting for a scrap, so I snuck him a piece of bacon.

As the missus cleared the dishes, Miller Johnson folded his arms on the table and looked at me like a proud papa. "No need to fear, Moses. I have transported many to safety. Did Joel tell thee about the wagon?"

"Yes sir. He said it has a hidin' place."

His face wrinkled up as he grinned. "Well, Moses, it's time I showed it to thee."

We walked out to the barn. A buckboard sat in the corner. The wagon wasn't no flatbed. It had sides all the way around that kept any load from falling out. Miller Johnson looked at it with a satisfied smile. He ran his hand across the smooth wood like he was patting a baby. "Come around to the back, and I'll show thee how it worketh."

The miller gripped the wagon's back plank with both hands like he was commencing some holy ritual. He jiggled it a bit and lifted the board right off.

I sucked in my breath. Hoo-wee. A hidey-hole big enough to hold a man appeared just like magic. No wonder the wagon box didn't look so deep. A fake bottom, just like Joel said. Miller Johnson slid the plank back down into special grooves along the wagon's sides. The little room disappeared. He poked his finger in a tiny hole at the bottom of the slat and pulled it up a bit. "When ye need more air, just push up the board a little." He patted my shoulder. "Ye shall be safe in here."

Uncle Hank told me the story once of how Buck hog-tied a runaway and stuck him in a box for two days. He almost died. I knowed this wagon box wasn't the same, but my hands was sweating anyway. I wiped them on my pants.

"How long this trip, sir?"

"Might take all day to reach Gettysburg, but around lunch time we should cross into Pennsylvania. My wife is packing food for thee. I'm sorry we cannot get thee out for some air, though, Moses." He frowned. "Slave catchers like to hang around the border looking for runaways."

Just the word runaway put my belly into a knot again. "Yes, sir."

He let Starlight out of her stall and hitched her up to the wagon. "Come on, girl."

"Gather thy things, Moses. We will leave as soon as we load the flour."

I climbed the ladder into the loft and grabbed my tote with the writing stick. I ran my fingers over my name one last time then went outside.

Miz Johnson hurried out to the buckboard carrying a basket of vittles with two hands. She parceled out two pieces of steaming cornbread and a slice of fatback into a bandanna, wrapped it up, and handed it to me. I stuck it in my tote. "Keep this with thee, Moses," she said. "No telling how long ye might be hiding in that box." She set the basket on the seat and turned to me with a most sorrowful look. She took my hands, blinking back tears. "How old art thou, Moses?"

I shook my head. "Don't rightly know, ma'am."

She reached up and stroked my head, even though I was a mite taller than she was. "Ye may be tall, but not much older than twelve, I'm guessing. And thy mother? Where might she be?"

I lowered my head. "Sold south, ma'am." She squeezed my hands. Her hands felt warm, like Mama's. "Doth she know ye hast run away?"

I choked on the words. "She helped me leave." Tears ran down my face. I wiped them away quick.

Miz Johnson's eyes got some spark back in them. She smiled. "That must make her so proud. Thy mother hath named thee well. Only a Moses would set out in the wilderness alone." She lifted a corner of her apron and wiped away the rest of my tears. "I will pray for thee, son."

"My mama is prayin' for me, too."

I helped Miller Johnson finish loading bags. The wagon bed was so shallow we had to lay the sacks sideways to fit them all in without them spilling over the top.

"Good job, Moses. Time to go." Miller Johnson slapped flour off his hands and walked to the back of the wagon. He pulled up the board. I tossed my tote into my new hidey-hole and crawled inside. He peeked in. "God be with thee." He dropped down the plank.

I lay on my side, curled up in a ball, and buried my head in my tote. For sure I didn't want the Johnson's to hear me bawling. It was daylight, but I was in the dark, just like when I walked to the mill. But a horse named Starlight was leading me, just like North Star led me. And this time I wasn't alone.

Chapter 10
The Border

All morning I shifted back and forth. About the time I got comfortable, the wagon would hit a rut and I'd bang my head on the false bottom. Felt worse than Zeke's feet in my back when we slept on the cabin floor. I got a cramp in my leg. Stretched it out as best I could in that tight space. I felt hot as stew in a pot, so I lifted the plank about an inch.

Just as I breathed in some fresh air, Miller Johnson said, "Whoa, easy girl."

We rolled to a stop. I heard hoof beats. Horses trotted toward us.

"Just be calm," he said to Starlight. I knowed he meant them words for me. I shut the plank quiet-like.

The clopping stopped. "Good day to thee," Miller Johnson said in a calm, but cheerful way.

A gruff voice spoke. "Good day to you, sir. I see you're headed across the Mason-Dixon line."

Another voice whispered. I couldn't make out the words.

The first voice spoke again. "Makin' a delivery?" He coughed. "Seems like a long way to bring a load of flour. They got plenty of mills in Pennsylvania."

The miller cleared his throat. "I am meeting the head master of the classical school in Gettysburg. I plan to purchase some textbooks from him and these goods are my payment."

"And what kind of goods would that be, sir?" He stretched out the word "goods" like he thought the miller was hiding something. He wheezed and chuckled at the same time. "Are you carryin' more than flour?"

"No sir. I am a miller by trade. I have no other goods."

"Well then, ya won't mind if we look around, will ya?"

"I have nothing to hide, but what right hast thee to search my wares?"

Somebody spit. More coughing. "We got papers from three slave owners in Frederick County offerin' a reward for the return of their property."

I felt sweat drip between my eyes and down my nose. My heart hammered against my ribs. Could they hear me breathing? I didn't dare move.

Somebody walked around the wagon. Slapped its sides. Thumped the flour sacks. I peeked through the little hole. He stood at the back of the wagon. Only thing between me and him was that board. He knocked on the plank. I bit my lip and tried not to shake.

The man with the cough spoke. "You know…folks that help slaves run away are breakin' the law."

"I am a law abiding man, sir." The miller paused. "Now that I think of it, someone reported a canoe missing not far from my mill. Perhaps ye might find someone paddling up the Monocacy River."

More grumbling and spitting. They walked away from the wagon. The two voices whispered to each other. One grunted. "I'll be watchin' for you next time you come this way, miller." The horses trotted away.

"May God watch over thee, gentlemen." Miller Johnson clucked at Starlight. "Come on, girl." The wagon rolled forward.

I lay on my belly and sobbed into my hands. My whole body shook like Buck had a hold of my neck, jerking me back and forth. Finally, them hands let go of me, and I went limp as a dishrag.

A bit of light poked through the hole, reminding me of North Star. I put my face next to the hole, and sucked in fresh air. My body started coming around. I was gonna live to see tomorrow.

I dozed off.

Chapter 11
Dobbin House

"Whoa, girl." Them words woke me up.

Another man spoke. "Miller Johnson, how good to see you. Bring that load right into the barn. We'll unpack it later." The wagon rolled a bit farther and came to a halt. The miller got down off the buckboard and walk around back. He jiggled the plank. The board slid up and bright light shined in, making me blink. Miller Johnson poked his smiling face inside my hidey-hole. He reached in and took a hold of my hand. "Welcome to Gettysburg, Moses."

I crawled out of that wagon box. Stood up too fast. Saw stars. I wobbled and stumbled. He grabbed me around my middle. "Put a hand on my shoulder, son. It might take thee a while to gain thy balance."

His shoulder felt steady. He led me gentle as a horseman with a light touch. My arms and legs got stronger as we walked toward the barn door. It sure felt good to plant my feet on the ground.

A man with a mustache waited by the door. He smiled, looking right eager to see us. He shook Miller Johnson's hand, then slicked back his dark, curly hair and shook my hand, too.

"Hello, I'm Matthew Dobbins. Come quickly. No slave catchers around now, but they have no shame. They can be trouble if they have legal documents." He tugged on his vest, turned on the heel of his black boot, and walked up the hill. We followed him.

A two-story stone house stood on the hill, tall and proper as a plantation mistress greeting company. The sight of that fine building near took my breath away.

I looked down the road. Didn't see no cotton or tobacco fields. No slaves or overseers. A garden and a few out buildings sat off to the side, but that was all. Miller Johnson took my arm. "It's a majestic house, and it is a school as well. But we must enter quickly."

"We in a free state now, ain't we?" I said as we walked through the door.

"Yes, but we are still too near the border for you to be safe," Mr. Dobbins said.

We entered the kitchen. Mr. Dobbins introduced us to his wife, Abigail, who stood at the wood stove stirring a pot. A couple of young 'uns clung on her skirt. A turkey was strung up from a rafter just above me. Two rabbit pelts hung on pegs by the fireplace. Wished I felt like eating, but my belly was still upset from the ride.

The missus rang a dinner bell. A white man and a black man walked in the room together, dressed in jackets and vests. Only time I ever seen a black man dressed so fine was if they was serving dinner at the Big House. Would he be serving the vittles? What if I was s'posed to help him? Ain't never waited on folks before.

I swallowed hard and looked at Miller Johnson.

"Fret thee not, Moses. These men are abolitionist friends."

Mr. Dobbins nodded to the white man and introduced us. "Meet lawyer and congressman, Thaddeus Stevens. He works to pass laws that outlaw slavery, and he defends fugitive slaves in the courts." He turned to the other man. "And this is Henry Butler. He has assisted many runaways to their next stop."

I didn't know what an abolitionist was, but Miller Johnson smiled and talked to them like they was kinfolk. If they helped slaves, in a way, I guess they was.

After we all sat down, Mr. Dobbins asked the miller how the trip went. He smiled, his eyes twinkling. "Moses and I had a close call, didn't we?"

I nodded. "Yessir."

Mrs. Dobbins poured him a cup of coffee. He took a sip and folded his hands on the table. "A couple of slave catchers approached us at the border. I thought for a moment they would find us out." He rolled his eyeballs up to the ceiling and cracked a smile. "Thank the Lord, I had a good reason to come to Pennsylvania." His smile stretched into a grin. "By the way, that story about the missing canoe is true. Several weeks ago we let a runaway take it upriver."

He explained the whole story, and everybody thought he was right clever. After the dishes got cleared away, they talked about where I was going next.

So much jabbering went on we almost didn't hear the knock at the door. Forks dropped. Everybody looked at me like I was a ghost. Mr. Dobbins stood up. "Abigail, go stall them until I get Moses upstairs. He took my arm.

We raced up the steps and stopped in the middle of the stairs. He ran his fingers along a wood panel in the wall, but it didn't look like nothing was there. Next thing I knowed, he slid open a secret door, like magic.

My eyes musta looked big as biscuits, 'cause Mr. Dobbins patted me on the shoulder. "Don't worry, Moses. No one can find you here. I'll come get you when it's safe." He helped me crawl into the dark little space. I took a deep breath. He shut the door.

My heart near thumped outta my chest. Here I was in another tight space and hardly room to breathe. But I could sit up, so I knew this hidey-hole was taller than the wagon box. My eyes got used to the dark. A small trunk sat next to me. I thought about climbing inside, but it was too small. I pressed my ear against the wall and listened for footsteps on the stairs.

Chapter 12
My Free Paper

I could hear folks jibber-jabbering downstairs, but it all sounded friendly-like. After awhile the front door banged shut and horses clip-clopped away. Somebody came up the stairs. The panel slid open.

Mr. Dobbins poked his nose in and grinned.

Sure made me feel better to see that smile.

"All's clear, Moses. You can come out now. Those were friends of ours. They came to warn us about some people who want to make trouble for us. Even in the north we have to be careful about our business. Not everybody wants to help runaways."

I nodded. "Yes sir." He offered me his hand. I climbed out.

We joined the others in the kitchen. I sat down between Miller Johnson and Henry. Mr. Dobbins stood at the end of the table and looked us up and down like Buck sizing up his work crew. He rested both hands on the table. "Here's the plan."

He spoke to Henry. "Tomorrow, Moses will accompany you when you take that load of feed up to Heidlersburg. Since that's only ten miles, I think you can push on to York Springs and spend the night with the Wrights. I sent word to Dr. Rutherford in Harrisburg that you are headed his way. He will know where you should travel from there."

Everybody nodded like they was satisfied with the plan. Mr. Thaddeus Stevens stood up.

He looked in my eyes, just like Miller Johnson did when I first met him. "You are a brave young man. I expect to hear good things about you someday. Do you know how to read?"

"No sir."

"Well, you will."

"Thank you, sir. I plan to, sir. Already, I can write my name, sir."

He turned up a corner of his mouth and winked. "You're off to a good start." He shook my hand strong. "If you all would excuse me, Henry is driving me home tonight. Don't worry, Moses. Henry will return for you tomorrow morning." He walked out of the room looking powerful as a bear. I still couldn't get used to a white man treating me like somebody. And such an important man as Mr. Stevens.

Mr. Dobbins made sleeping arrangements for me and the miller. Everybody thought I should sleep in the secret room to be safe. Mr. Dobbins pulled a blanket out of the chest for me. I was mighty thankful for it. It wasn't no tick, but it was better than lying on the hard floor. Mr. Dobbins and Miller Johnson bid me goodnight. They shut the secret door.

The next morning at breakfast, Mr. Dobbins toted in a pile of books and plunked them on the table. He picked out two and held them out to Miller Johnson. "I think you'll appreciate these."

The miller's eyes lit up like them books was a slice of fresh apple pie. "I've wanted a McGuffey Reader and dictionary a long time now. Joel will appreciate these."

He bid us all farewell and lugged his pile of books out to the wagon.

I asked Mr. Dobbins, "You think I could see the miller off? Is it safe?"

"I believe so, Moses. Go ahead."

I ran out to the buckboard. "Thank you, Mr. Johnson. I'm beholden to you for your kindness."

He smiled like a papa. "Thou art welcome, son. May God protect thee and those who guide thee." I blinked back tears. Looked away. Ain't never had a white man be so good to me.

Just as Miller Johnson rode off, Henry Butler pulled up in his wagon. He hopped off, walked back to the wagon box and patted a large oak desk that lay on its side. "I gotta deliver this here desk to Reverend and Mrs. Palmer in Harrisburg."

I ran my hand across the smooth wood. The desk had lots of little drawers with shiny knobs.

Henry smiled big like we was going on a Sunday picnic instead of making a dangerous trip. "Remember the plan, Mose? We stop at the stable first then go to the Wrights' house where we'll put up for the night. Get your stuff. This train is bound for glory." He chuckled and slapped the desk.

I ran back in the house and grabbed my tote.

When I came back, Henry said, "Don't want this fine piece of furniture getting scratched up. Help me load bags of horse feed around it, will you, Mose?"

Mr. Dobbins came outside to see us off. Didn't take his eyes off me. He looked like a proud papa as he reached in his vest pocket and handed me a piece of paper. "This very legal-looking document, Moses, declares you are a free person of color."

Them words about knocked the breath outta me. I dropped the paper but snatched it back before it hit the ground. "Sorry, sir." I stared at the paper, wishing I could read what it said. "A free paper? Is it real, sir?"

He grinned like a tomcat that just caught hisself a bird. "No, Moses. It's a fake. But a very good fake."

He tapped his finger on my paper. "This should make your trip to Harrisburg a lot easier. Would you like to ride on the seat next to Henry?"

I swallowed. "Yes-s, sir." I clapped my hands together. "Thank you, sir."

Lordy, I was gonna be riding high in broad daylight. Breathing fresh air instead of snuffling in a hidey-hole. No disrespect to my hidey-holes. They was getting me where I needed to go. I was right thankful for them. But I was even more thankful to be ridin' in the sunshine. Have somebody to talk to. I jumped up on that buckboard wearing a big grin.

Henry winked at me as he clucked to the horse. "Come on."

We started down the road.

I ran a hand across the wooden seat. Back on the plantation, I used to help Uncle Hank load corn in the wagon. Masta Bill always gave him a pass so he could take stuff to market. He let me hold his pass once. I couldn't read it, but I knew it said he had Master's say-so to go off the plantation. I had something a whole lot better than Uncle Hank's pass. I had a ticket to freedom.

I ran a finger over the words and hunted for my name in the middle of all them scribbles. The letters was strung together in swirls, and looked a lot different than the letters Joel taught me, so I couldn't find an "M."

I asked Henry, "Do you know how to read?"

He laughed. "I can write my name, like you, but I always been too busy workin' to get schoolin'."

I folded my free paper and stuck it in my shirt pocket. "That so?"

"I own the livery stable in Heidlersburg where we're taking the feed. It's right on the Harrisburg road. I carry a lot of freight, too, like this here desk."

If you don't mind my asking, "I guess you always been free?"

"Yep. My pappy was free, too. Slavery's been illegal in Pennsylvania for a long time."

We chatted some more about his family…and how he earned the money to buy his business.

But another question was stirring my innards. My free paper looked all fancy and proper. Whoever done it did a fine job. But who? I rubbed my forehead. "You got any idea who wrote this for me? I was thinkin' Mr. Stevens, him bein' a lawyer and all."

Henry turned up one corner of his mouth and kept looking straight ahead. "Cain't say I do." He winked at me. "But I do know folks who write them kinda documents don't let on who they are, 'cause they'd get in a heap of trouble."

I nodded. I figured Mr. Stevens wrote it. He probably made free papers for other folks, too.

Sun still hung high in the sky when we reached Henry's livery. It stood like a fine wood house on the edge of town. We parked in front and unloaded the feed sacks. The place smelled like fresh hay and oiled leather. Harnesses and bridles hung on posts. Men stood around the stalls, gabbing about goings on in town, some of them boarding horses, some of them looking to rent one. And them fine, sleek animals stood about, their smooth coats shining like stars.

We watered the horses, grabbed some vittles and started down the road with Reverend Palmer's desk. Henry said we'd be in York Springs before nightfall and get to Harrisburg the next day.

"Is the Reverend a white man?" I asked.

"Yep. But he's an abolitionist. He's put up many a slave at his place."

I nodded. I was glad I was staying with the doctor. Didn't much like white preachers. On the plantation, Reverend Sully always went on about how God gave us our masters. He said if we didn't obey, we was disobeying God, and God would whup us worse in the next world than our masters did here if we didn't repent.

Mama told me that was a bunch of trash. With fire in her eyes, she said, "Ol' Sully talk with his mouth and say nothin'. Jesus tol' me to talk with my heart. The Bible say Moses was a slave, and God set him free. Well, my heart tol' me that was right."

Well, I say Mama's heart knows better than Ol' Sully's mouth.

Chapter 13
Across the River

William and Phoebe Wright took us in that night. They was Quaker folks like Miller Johnson. They looked after me like I was kin and loaded us down with bread and bacon for the trip. Miz Wright cried a little, rubbed my head, and prayed for me. Just like Miz Johnson prayed. I figured all Quaker women did that.

Henry and I set off on the Harrisburg Road. About an hour later, black clouds rolled across the sky, and sure enough, by lunchtime, rain poured like a flood. Henry spied a barn not too far off and hightailed it until we got there. The door stood open, and we drove right in.

Henry jumped off the buckboard. He slapped his wet hat against his leg and walked around back to check the wagonload. "Could be worse, I s'pose. At least we got some shelter. But somehow I gotta dry off this wet wood. Otherwise this desk is gonna warp."

I spied some rags piled next to a stall and helped Henry dry off the desk. When the rain stopped, we started back down the road, thanking the Lord we didn't get into trouble with whoever owned that barn.

Sun showed up and my shirt started to dry. I reached in my pocket for my paper. It felt damp. I pulled it out and opened it.

Wet ink ran right down the middle, smearing the words all together. I couldn't make out a single letter. And here I was, riding high in daylight where some slaver might see me.

I looked back at the wagon box. I couldn't hide back there with bags of feed piled around that desk. No hidey-hole for me on this trip. My hands started sweating.

Henry looked over at me. "You don't look so good. What ailin' you, Mose?"

I held my paper up and spit out the words. "Look! Ain't nothin' left to read! What if we get stopped?"

Henry frowned and pulled up on the reins. We stopped on the side of the road. "Let me see that, Mose." He shook his head. "Yep. Cain't use this no more."

I folded it and stuffed it back in my pocket. "I wish I never left home. My Uncle Hank told me anybody who runs is a fool. I shoulda I listened to him."

He put his hand on my shoulder. "Now, now. Settle down. Let me think about this. I'm sorry 'bout your paper. I really am. But we gotta stay calm. Cain't act like somethin's wrong. We just gotta pray. Runnin' is dangerous business, but the Lord is on our side." He rubbed his chin. "Sit up straight. Hold your head high. Pretend like you a free man just out for a fine ride." He smiled. "Come on, now. Let me see you smile, too."

I stretched my mouth into a grin, but my belly twisted into a knot.

I did just like Henry said. Every time we passed somebody I nodded and smiled, just like I was free.

We came upon a river. It rested all sleepy and quiet like the one by Miller Johnson's, but was so wide you couldn't throw a rock across it. The longest bridge I ever seen reached across it like a skinny black arm. My mouth dropped open.

Henry chuckled. "Better watch now, or you gonna catch some flies."

I smiled. "How you know that's what my mama always say?"

He pointed. "That there is the Susquehanna River. Harrisburg's on the other side."

Lord in heaven, I wasn't expecting we'd have to cross no bridge. It looked like one heavy load could snap it like a twig. I watched a carriage come across and it did just fine. But would it hold up a load like ours?

Henry clucked at the horse and we started across.

I looked way down at the brown water. That knot in my belly got so tight I could hardly breathe. I closed my eyes and listened to the wagon rumble over them wooden planks. They clacked like the bones the slaves used to play when they got together to whoop it up on Saturday nights. I opened my eyes when the clacking stopped.

At the end of the bridge, a man walked out of a shed.

"We gotta pay a toll for goin' over the bridge," Henry told me. He reached in his pocket and gave the man some money. The man looked us over suspicious-like.

"You got free papers?" he said to me. I held out the wet paper. I took a deep breath and gave him my best smile. "Got caught in a rainstorm."

The man winked at Henry. "He's one of your shipments, ain't he?" He handed the money back. "No charge for that kinda freight."

I put my paper in my pocket and let out my breath.

Henry tipped his hat. "Much obliged, Mordecai."

Henry grinned. I smiled back. This time my smile was real.

We rolled into Harrisburg—the first city I ever laid eyes on. I saw shops and houses crowded next to each other and streets running every which way filled with horses, carts, and people.

Henry leaned next to me. "Dr. Rutherford lives just a block away on Front Street.

He treats everybody the same, rich or po', black or white. He's president of the Anti-slavery Society. He has a whole lotta black friends—and a few white enemies." We turned down a narrow street.

A man like that had school smarts. Maybe the doctor could make me a new free paper.

Chapter 14
Trouble

We parked outside a two-story house. Henry found a boy to watch our stuff for a nickel. We walked into the parlor. A couch and some padded chairs sat there looking a lot like the fancy furniture at the Big House on Oakley Plantation. I didn't dare sit on none of it.

Upstairs, somebody moaned like he was hurting bad.

We heard a man say, "Now just hold still."

I peeked out the parlor entrance and looked up the steps. There was drops of blood going all the way up the stairs. A shiver ran down my back. Henry musta seen I was scared. He took a look for himself. His eyes popped wide open. He held a finger to his lips to let me know not to say nothing.

I stood by the doorway while he poked around the rooms on the first floor. He grabbed my arm and took me into the kitchen. Sat me in a chair. "Stay here till I find out what's goin' on." He walked upstairs.

I started to sweat. I wanted to bolt out the back door and just start running. But where would I go? I tried to listen to the talk going on but couldn't make out the words. I put my hands up to the kitchen window and stared through the glass. Houses and other buildings was crowded together. I knew I could run between them quicker than a rabbit—if I had to make a getaway.

I heard feet clomp down the stairs. I grabbed the door latch. Waited.

"Make sure you see Pap in a few days so he can check that bullet wound."

"Thanks, Doc. I dunno what folks in Tanner's Alley would do without you 'n Pap." The door shut.

Henry walked into the kitchen with a tall white man in a vest with his shirtsleeves rolled up past his elbows. His hands were covered in blood like he just gutted a deer. He held a bullet between his fingers.

I swallowed hard.

Henry grabbed a pitcher of water and poured it into a washbasin.

"Thanks, Henry," the doctor said. He dropped the bullet in the basin and washed his hands.

A white woman in a gray dress and apron toted a pail of dirty water into the kitchen. She opened the back door and dumped it outside. A black man followed right behind her, carrying a bundle of bloody rags. He tossed them in a big washtub on the floor.

"I'll have supper on in a minute," the woman said.

The doctor sat down and rested his elbows on the table. He rubbed his eyes. "I'm afraid these folks don't have time for supper, Eleanor. Could you get them some bread to take on the road? And maybe some jerky?"

She nodded. "I'll do my best."

Henry said, "Dr. Rutherford. This here is Moses."

The doctor shook my hand and motioned for me and Henry to sit down. The man who carried the rags sat next to the doctor. "Let me introduce you folks to Pap," the doctor said. "This is my good friend and fellow conductor on the Underground Railroad, Pap Jones." He looked him in the eye like a proud papa looks at a son.

Pap Jones reached across the table and shook my hand. "Glad to meet you, Moses."

The doctor went on. "Pap is a leader in the Harrisburg black community. The other day a family of slaves showed up at my office. A couple and two small children. I sent them over to Pap to put up in his barn over in Tanner's Alley. The fellow I just treated, Sam, heard folks over at the barbershop say they saw two strange men check in at the hotel. They were pretty sure they were slave catchers. Pap organized the neighbors to protect the fugitives."

Pap bowed his head like he wasn't used to being bragged on. He held up a hand, like he was telling the doc enough's been said, but the doctor paid him no mind.

"When the sheriff heard about it, he rounded up the local militia to go after the neighbors. They disbanded as soon as they heard the militia coming, but the thugs went after them anyway. They brandished pistols, invaded homes, and arrested all the darkies they could find." Dr. Rutherford shook his head. "Just because a black man is free doesn't mean he's treated right by the lawmen in town." He looked at Pap Jones. "They shot Sam in the arm. Pap and I removed the bullet. Sam will be okay." He half smiled. "The good news is—the fugitive family got away."

Dr. Rutherford picked up the bullet and rolled it between his fingers. He looked over at me kinda sorrowful, then closed his eyes and shook his head. "I don't think it's safe for you around here now."

I swallowed. "Yessir."

He gave Henry a nod. "You have freight to deliver?"

"Yessir. I got a desk for Reverend Palmer."

Dr. Rutherford wrinkled his brow. "I have a piece of canvas we could tie over the wagon bed. Moses, can you hide under that?"

I sat up straight. "Yep. I done hid in smaller places."

He slapped the table. "Good." He turned to Henry. "Take your load straight to the Palmers' farmhouse. I think they will take Moses in. His church has harbored a few runaways."

We all shook hands. Henry went outside and paid the boy watching the wagon.

Sun was bedding down for the night when we started down the road. Less chance that anybody see us at night. I opened my tote and bit off a piece of jerky. It was a right scary day, but I told myself I had lots to be thankful for. I had vittles for the trip and folks helping me. But with all the commotion, I forgot to ask the doctor to make me a free paper. Maybe I could ask the white preacher. But only if he'd be willing to look me in the eye. Maybe I could trust him then.

Chapter 15
The Palmers

Wasn't long before the wagon stopped. Wasn't near as long a trip as the one from the mill to Gettysburg. I lifted up the cover just a bit and peeked out.

Henry climbed down and walked around back to unload the desk. A tall white man with gray hair and a well-trimmed beard walked out of the house to greet him. He wore a black coat with a preacher's white collar. I figured he must be the Reverend.

He slapped the desk. "Mighty fine, Henry. Mighty fine. But let's get our guest settled before we take this in the house." He and Henry untied the cover. He offered me his hand. "I'm Reverend Palmer. You must be Moses."

"Yes, sir. Glad to meet you."

He helped me crawl out of the wagon box, all the time looking me in the eye. He smiled like a preacher—didn't show no teeth and looked right through me like he knew all my secrets. But he didn't look down on me all suspicious-like, thinking I gonna run away any minute, like Preacher Sully did. Did that mean I could trust him?

"Let's get you down to the cellar. Sorry I can't provide better lodging, but we might have people stop by the house. Not everyone in the North is anti-slavery."

He pulled open a cellar door. It made a whining sound that gave me the shivers.

He waved me over. "All right, come on now."

But when I caught sight of that doorway, I froze like a scared rabbit. That cellar stood open like a giant mouth.

Henry grabbed my arm. "There ain't no ghosts down there, Mose. Trust me." He pulled me down into the cellar's belly.

I blinked and waited for my eyes to get used to the light. Baskets of green beans, cauliflower, and turnips sat next to the dirt wall. Jars of jam sat on an old sideboard with a drawer missing. A tick and a blanket lay on a pile of straw on the floor. Henry was right. The place seemed right friendly. I had no reason to be scared. Why, this just another hidey-hole.

"Make yo'self at home," Henry said. "The Reverend and I will be back after I unload that desk."

I fell on that bed like it was Mama's arms. It smelled like fresh straw and felt soft and fine as the one in Miller Johnson's loft. I didn't lie there very long before the door opened.

Henry clomped down the stairs. Two women clutching their skirts climbed down after him. One was young, pretty, and black. She hid behind a white lady holding a candle.

Henry took off his hat. "This here is Miz Palmer, the wife of Reverend Palmer."

The Missus handed Henry the candle and took my hands. Her smile was as soft as her fingers. She wore a dress the color of the sky with a white collar. It didn't look fancy like the dresses Master's wife, Miz Oakley, wore. It smelled clean like soap. A ruffled cap covered her brown hair, but the gray streak above her ears poked through.

Henry turned to the black woman. "And this here is Tillie."

A smile stretched across Tillie's face. She had teeth white as milk, and her dark eyes sparkled like stars. I figured she was a couple of years older than me. Didn't carry herself like a growed woman but had started to look like one. She smoothed out her apron and fiddled with her head wrap. "Lordy, lordy," she said, shaking her head. "You awful young to be settin' out by yo'self." She looked up and rolled her eyeballs. "Thank the Lord you got this far."

Miz Palmer still had a hold of my hands. "Are you hungry?"

Her voice sounded sweet as honey. I cleared my throat. "Yes'm."

"Tillie, would you bring Moses down a bowl of vegetable soup?" She turned to Henry. "Would you stay for supper? We can put you up for the night. It's starting to get dark."

He plunked his hat on his head. "Thank you, ma'am, but I'll be headin' to my brother's place over in Tanner's Alley." He nodded. "Much obliged, though. Thank you for the invite." He smiled at me.

"I know the Missus here will take right good care. May the Lord watch over you, Moses."

"Thanks, Henry." I shook his hand and watched him climb up the cellar stairs.

As soon as he left, Tillie came down, trying to steady a bowl of soup in her hands. Reverend Palmer followed her.

I pulled my free paper out of my pocket and unfolded it. It had dried a long time ago. I felt the smudges. They were dry, too.

"What have you got there?" he asked.

"My free paper, sir. It ain't real, sir. Besides, it got rained on. Ain't any good now." I handed it to him.

He wrinkled his brow and ran a finger over the smudges. "How did you get this?"

I told him the story of Mr. Dobbins and Mr. Thaddeus Stevens.

He chuckled. "Thaddeus Stevens has no fear." He handed me my paper.

"Don't s'pose there's anything we can do about this, sir?"

He shook his head and frowned. "Afraid not, son. Mr. Stevens is the only one I know who could help you with this."

I looked at the ground. "Yes, sir. Thank you, sir." Didn't want him to see I was disappointed. Wished I hadn't got my hopes up.

"I'm so sorry, Moses." Mrs. Palmer took hold of my hand and the Reverend's arm at the same time. "Jonathon, must we send the boy to the next stop tomorrow? I would love to see him get some rest."

He frowned and rubbed his chin. "You know they just had trouble in the city."

Tillie folded her hands like she was praying. But she didn't close her eyes. She begged with them. Her big brown eyes looked just like a doe's. "Sir, could he please stay with us a spell? I could say he's my brother, and Mama sent him here to help out." She turned to Mrs. Palmer. "And ain't you lookin' for a farm hand to help bring in them crops?"

Miz Palmer's cheeks turned rosy. Her smile changed to a grin. "That I am."

"I knew it, I knew it. Why, Moses here is just the kinda help you been lookin' for." Tillie's eyes got bigger, and bigger. Just when I thought them eyeballs might pop right out of her head she said, "Oh, oh…he could take lessons with us in the afternoons."

Miz Palmer stared at Tillie like somebody just surprised her with a box of chocolates. "Oh, what a fine idea. I would love to have another student." She turned to her husband. "Could we, Jonathan? It's been two years since we took in Tillie, and no one's suspected she's a runaway." She and Tillie both gave him them doe eyes.

His frown melted into a smile. "I can't refuse you, Sarah." He wrapped an arm around her middle. "But we must be very careful."

"Yes sir." I tried to say so all respectful-like, but my insides was dancing.

Tillie opened a door in the sideboard and reached inside. "Miz Palmer…may I?"

"Oh, what a wonderful idea."

My eyes musta looked big as Tillie's. Tillie pulled out a slate and a piece of chalk, just like I seen Masta Bill's son, Billy, use for his lessons. That sideboard didn't have no dishes. It was a special hidey-hole for schooling.

Miz Palmer turned to me. "This cellar is our schoolhouse. Would you to like to learn to read and write, Moses?"

"I…I'd be grateful for the chance, ma'am." I picked up my tote and wrapped the strap around my finger. "I already learned my name."

The Reverend's smile grew bigger. "Well done, son. Can you show us?"

Tillie held out the chalk and slate.

"Much obliged, but I ain't never used chalk. If you don't mind, I'd rather use my stick."

I pulled out my writing stick and drew my name on the ground. When I looked up, I saw nothing but smiles and eyes that shined like stars. Mrs. Palmer blinked and a tear trickled down her cheek. She wrapped her arms around me in a big hug.

Mind you, she didn't have no pillow arms like Mama, but it was a nice hug, just the same—one Mama would be proud of.

Chapter 16
The Fugitive Slave Act

Two weeks went by faster than Big Times at Christmas. One afternoon, Tillie and I sat on the cellar floor doing lessons after we done chores. Baskets of corn, beans, and other stuff we picked lay stacked around us.

I steadied my slate on my knees and copied everything she showed me. I had learned two new letters every day and was right proud of myself. Now I could write the whole alphabet and sound out each letter.

Tillie taught me by candlelight, but if folks wasn't snooping around, we'd go up to the house and get a reading lesson from Miz Palmer.

"It takes more than running away to be free," Miz Palmer told us one day, waving a book in her hand. "Your mind needs to be free, too."

"Pardon me, ma'am, but how you do that? It seems to me my mind's all locked up inside my head."

Tillie giggled. "She ain't talkin' 'bout your mind flyin' around like a bird, Mose. She talkin' about how all the stuff we been learnin' teaches you to take care of yo'self. Don't need no masta givin' you food if you can make your own money. You can decide where to live and where to work."

Miz Palmer looked at Tillie like a proud mama. "Well put, my girl, well put."

I shoulda known. I was already starting to feel free on the inside. And ain't that what I said about Mama that day they snatched her away? But she didn't need no book learning to get free. Her mind got free the day she knew her boy wasn't gonna be a slave no more.

We heard clip-clopping coming up the road.

Tillie jumped up and opened the drawer. "Put your school stuff away, Mose', and grab some vegetables to bring up to the house. It's the Reveren', I'm sure. But we gotta be careful."

I slid my slate under the tick, and Tillie stuck the alphabet papers in the drawer of the sideboard. We raced up the cellar stairs and tore past the horse and carriage parked in front of the house. We ran up the porch steps.

Mr. Palmer got out of the coach dressed in his black coat and top hat—what he always wore for town meetings. He caught sight of us and waved us into the house. His eyes burned like hot coals.

Tillie and I looked at each other. We wondered what made him so mad. I hoped it wasn't me.

He marched in the house and slammed his hat on the dining room table. "They did it, Sarah, they finally did it."

Miz Palmer rushed into the room. Her face turned white as chalk. "What is it, Jonathan?"

He ran his fingers through his hair. "Those fools in Congress passed the Fugitive Slave Act."

Miz Palmer sat down at the table and buried her head in her arms. "Lord, have mercy."

I looked from the Reverend to the Missus. Tillie shifted from one foot to the other and fiddled with her head wrap. Her eyes got big. "What you mean, Reveren'? Do we gotta leave?" She rolled the edges of her apron between her fingers.

He motioned for us to sit down, sighed and rubbed his eyes. "Pennsylvania lawmen have never been required to arrest slaves and return them to their owners. Many courts wouldn't even convict escaped slaves. Now the U.S. government says we have to assist slave catchers or risk paying a thousand dollar fine. Not only that, anyone who feeds or houses an escaped slave is subject to that same fine and six months in prison."

Miz Palmer ran into the kitchen sobbing.

"Sarah, come in here. You need to hear this," he said.

She walked into the dining room, drying her eyes with her apron.

He put an arm around her and made himself smile. "We will go through this together." He gave her a squeeze. "God is with us. But I'm worried about the sheriff. After all, he tried to stop the folks in

Tanner's Alley from helping that fugitive family. He could very well turn in anyone he knows who helps slaves."

Tillie's hands shook. Her lip trembled. "Well, then—we gotta leave right away. I cain't let nobody do that to you."

Miz Palmer hugged her like a mama bear with her cub. She tucked a loose hair back under her wrap. "There, there, Tillie. You're not alone. We will help you and Moses." She looked at Reverend Palmer. "Right, Jonathan?"

He smacked the table. "Yes." He shook his head. "But it's not safe for you here anymore. We will help you get to Canada."

Tillie let out a little cry.

Miz Palmer stroked her cheek. "There, there, you're going to get me crying, too. I hate to see you go." She looked at the Reverend with sad eyes. "We have to do what is best. The sheriff knows you live here. I couldn't live with myself if he came and took you." She threw her arms around Tillie.

It was a sorrowful day for sure. Just watching Miz Palmer and Tillie about broke my heart. Far as I know, Miz Palmer never had no young 'uns of her own, and she been treating Tillie like her own kin for two years now. I only been here two weeks but I felt like I was leaving family, too.

Who would take care of us now? Maybe Tillie and I be looking out for each other.

When Tillie settled down, Miz Palmer came over and hugged me tight. I could barely breathe. Miz Palmer blinked to hold back them tears, but one ran down her cheek anyway, just like one ran down my mama's face that morning I ran away.

I wanted to cry, but I wanted to be brave more—just like I was brave for Mama. And here I was again—leaving home, and getting ready to run away.

Chapter 17
Preparations

The next day the Reverend rode off to another meeting. The Missus looked all misty-eyed. Her chin shook, and she twisted her apron around her finger as she watched him go. I thought she was gonna bust out crying again, but instead, she put her arms around us like a hen fussing over baby chicks and told us not to fret. The Reverend would talk to other conductors and find out where we was going next. "In the meantime, you keep busy." She put us to chores around the place. Tillie scrubbed the floors, and I split logs for firewood.

I ain't never heard it so quiet. Tillie didn't babble on or run around about this and that. Miz Palmer didn't hum and sing like she always do. I tried to sing a work song to cheer myself up but the words wouldn't come. That horrible sad silence just smothered it. I only heard my axe—whack, whack. Cracking like a gunshot.

Tillie lugged a pail of wash water down the front porch steps and tossed it in the flowerbed. She came running over. "Missus said to tell you about them work boots that belong to the Reveren'."

I put down the axe. "What boots?"

"Why the ones he's givin' you, that's what." She shook her head. "Missus say you cain't be runnin' away without no shoes." She ran back in the house and came back with a pair of black leather work boots. "Here." She pushed them into my hands. "See if they fit."

I sat on the ground and pulled them on. I hadn't worn a pair of shoes since last winter. They was a little big, but felt good and broke in. And not too small. I wouldn't get any blisters. Sweet heaven. Ain't that just like the Lord to give the Reverend the notion to give me these boots. I was gonna thank him.

Miz Palmer came out and swept the porch. "I think it's time for a break. Why don't you two get in a lesson while you can?" She looked around. Then shooed us into the cellar.

All that sadness waited outside as we went down to our hidey-hole school and shut the door. Tillie's eyes brightened. We pulled out the slates and chalk like nothing had changed. Tillie wrote down some words, and I copied them on my slate. But then she put down her chalk and looked at the sideboard. She stared at me. Her mind was stirring like a butter churn. She looked back at the sideboard again.

"Well, I was gonna wait to show you this, but since we ain't gonna be here...." She tugged on a strip of wood above the drawer on the sideboard. She jiggled it, but it didn't have a mind to move. "Blame it all, loosen up now, will ya?" She dug under it with her fingernails. Doggone if it didn't come loose. She pulled out a skinny drawer.

I clapped my hand over my mouth. That sideboard had a secret hidey-hole. I looked inside. Paper, white as cream, and real pencils.

"We gonna use this stuff today. It may be our last chance." She handed me a paper and pencil like they was gold. "What you write on this you get to keep. Don't have to erase it like no slate."

I rubbed the paper between my fingers. It felt smooth as an oak leaf. I rolled the pencil back and forth. I wanted to try it out somehow before I wrote on that fine paper. Didn't want to make no mistakes. I marked my hand with the letter M. The pencil made a skinny gray line on my palm. I rubbed it off with my finger. I could write smaller with a pencil than I could with chalk.

I laid the paper on top of my slate. "What you gonna write about, Tillie?"

"I'm writin' a thank you to the Missus and Reveren'." She shook her head. "They help me so much.... I pray nothin' bad happens to 'em."

I nodded. I was gonna thank them, too. Already I been thinking of words I want to tell them. But what did I want to write?

Sometimes Miz Palmer read to us from a newspaper abolitionists printed. People wrote about how wrong slavery is, and how slaves got a right to be free. Them words fired me up like a match on kindling. Lots of folks got to see them words. I reckon them words fired up lots of folks.

"Do we got one of them abolitionist papers in the cellar?" I asked Tillie.

"No. They be up at the house." She cocked her head sideways. "You wanna be a 'bolitionist?"

I dodged her stare and shrugged my shoulders. "Naw. I ain't smart enough."

She put a hand on her hip. "And what you think Miz Palmer might say about that? How many times she say—ain't nothin' a white man can do that a black man cain't." She shook her pencil at me. "You wanna be a writer? I can see you writin' for that 'bolitionist paper right now. Keep learnin' and you can do it."

There she went and said what I didn't have the gumption to believe. That voice in my head kept telling me no black boy should even think them words. It's one thing to want to be free. It's a whole different story to act high and mighty like you somebody special. I know what Reverend Sully would say. He'd say that ain't nothing but pride. Black folks got to know their place. I put down the pencil and closed my eyes.

What would Mama say? All of a sudden, them words she spoke at the train station popped into my head. "You gonna lead our people someday, jus' like Moses in the Bible." I never took in them words before. Maybe I was too broke up about Mama leaving. Now they felt like a fire burning in my belly.

"Tillie. I know what I wanna write."

"Yeah?"

"I'm gonna write about freedom."

Her eyes grew big. She patted the ground next to her. "Set next to me. I'll help you with the big words."

A pencil was harder to hold than chalk, but if I was gonna learn to write for a newspaper, then I was gonna learn how to write with a pencil. I squeezed my fingers around it and wrote slow and careful.

My name is Moses. My mama named me that because she wanted me to be free. Now I am. I don't work in the fields no more. I can earn my own pay. I can marry who I want. My children will never be slaves. Someday I will tell them what it was like to be a slave and how important it is to be free.

Tillie held what I wrote next to the candle. We both read it together. She blinked back a tear. "My, my, them's fine words. That be your first freedom newspaper. Bless God, may it be the first of many."

I shook my head. "This ain't no real newspaper."

"Oh yeah? When other people read it, then I reckon it will be."

She got me thinking like my mama again. Maybe someday I was gonna write in ink. With a quill pen. Just like Mr. Thaddeus Stevens wrote my free paper.

We heard the carriage rumble up to the house. The Missus threw open the cellar door, all out of breath. "Come quickly. There's no time to waste."

Tillie grabbed my paper and shoved it with hers in the secret drawer. I watched the first paper I ever wrote disappear into a hidey-hole where nobody might see it ever. We ran up the cellar steps.

Chapter 18
A Scary Getaway

The Missus hurried us both into the house.

Mr. Palmer sat in the parlor counting coins. "Tillie, these are your wages for the week and some extra for your journey." He turned to me. "Moses, I am paying you for your work harvesting the crops." He dropped the money into two small sacks, pulled the drawstrings, and handed them to us.

I rolled the bag around in my hand. It felt heavy and made a clinking sound. I stuck my hand in the bag and pulled out a hard, smooth coin. First time I ever got to hold money. I rubbed my finger over the picture of a lady in a fine dress. She held a flag. It musta been nighttime in the picture because a row of stars sat above her head. Maybe she been following stars, too.

The Reverend sat with his eyes closed and hands folded. I had a feeling he was praying. He looked up at me and Tillie. The tiredness was gone and fire filled up them eyes. "We have to make plans for your escape. After dark, I will drive you both to a barbershop in Harrisburg. The owner, William Goodridge, is a former slave. He also owns a railroad and transports fugitives. You'll board his train and ride to western Pennsylvania. Folks there can help you get to Erie. Then it's just a boat ride to Canada." He rubbed his brow. "If, for some reason, I am arrested…." He pointed to the back door. "You run through the woods as fast as you can. Head toward the city, but stay off the roads. The canal runs through the center of town. The towpath will take you up to Williamsport. "Gather your things. We leave at sunset."

"Yes, sir." I looked at Tillie. I hoped she knew what he was talking about. What was a canal? What was a towpath? How we know what to look for? I hoped we could ride in his carriage to that railroad car. As much as I hated trains, I wanted somebody to help us on our trip. Didn't want to walk in the middle of night, in the middle of nowhere, with nobody to help us.

I fetched my tote out of the kitchen, and folded up the cover I been sleeping on. I started to put it in Mrs. Palmer's blanket chest but she stopped me. "You keep it, Moses. It's going to get cold soon, and you'll need it if you're sleeping outside."

"Thank you, ma'am." I rolled it and put it next to my tote.

She brought out biscuits, fatback, and apples—and tried to smile. Tillie and I was grateful, but didn't know what to say. We stuffed the food in our bags.

I stepped out onto the porch. Sun hung right under the trees. It wouldn't be long before that big orange ball would sink into the ground.

I heard a noise. Men riding horses came out of the woods. My gut froze. I ran into the house. "Reverend Palmer, Reverend Palmer. Three men is comin' up the road."

Miz Palmer put an arm around us both and scooted us into the kitchen. "You listen real good. If these men come inside, run to the outhouse. If they arrest Jonathan, head for the towpath." A tear ran down her cheek. She wiped it away. "I may never see you again,

but…know that I love you both." She shut the kitchen door and rushed into the parlor.

Tillie and I hunkered down by the back door. We heard voices outside. Loud. Angry.

Somebody pounded on the front door. *Bam, bam, bam.*

Miz Palmer screamed. "Don't break it!"

The voices got louder. They were in the parlor. "I know you been hidin' runaways. Now where are they?"

Tillie grabbed my arm. Her fingers felt like ice. I held my breath and put my hand on the doorknob.

"You won't find any fugitives here, sheriff. Why don't you just go," Mr. Palmer said firmly.

"Very funny, Reverend. A man of the cloth like you should be obeyin' the law. Don't you know there's a fine for hidin' slaves?"

"Like I said, you won't find any slaves here."

"Then you won't mind us lookin' around, will you?"

Tillie and I bolted out the back door and hid behind the outhouse. We heard the men searching the house. They walked outside and opened the cellar door. I prayed they wouldn't find that secret drawer in the sideboard.

Tillie and me figured it was safer inside the outhouse. She opened the door. It creaked like a rooster waking the farm. We both snuck in and hoped they didn't hear us. Footsteps came close. I held my breath. We flattened up against the walls. An eye stared through the knothole in the door. Just when I thought somebody would open it, a man said, "Come on, Joe, they ain't here."

The feet walked away. I let out my breath and sank to the floor.

"So Reverend," another man said, "you already sent them on their way, huh? We'll find 'em. You know, Richard McAllister is settin' up a Slave Commission office. He'll help us send these darkies back where they belong."

After they grumbled and shuffled around some we heard them gallop away.

I pushed open the door real careful-like and tiptoed out. My legs felt wobbly. I sucked in the fresh air. Smelling that stink made my eyes water. We sat on the ground.

"Lordy, Lordy, we made it through this one," Tillie said.

I wiped my eyes. "Never thought I'd thank God for a stinkin' outhouse."

I spotted Mrs. Palmer bent over, sneaking toward us.

She knelt down and took Tilllie's hand. "I'm so sorry you had to go through this." She took my hand, too. "I think the safest thing…is for you to go. Now." She looked at Tillie with sorrowful eyes. "How can I let you go? You've been like a daughter…. Dare I even say that?" She buried her face in her hands. "Let me pray for you." She wrapped her arms around us like she'd never let go. "Lord, help these two precious lambs find their way to Canada. Keep them safe and out of harm's way on their journey." She held onto us a mite longer then lowered her arms. "I have to let you go."

Them sad eyes turned fiery. "Head toward the city. You'll see the towpath when you reach the canal. You remember where it is, don't you, Tillie? Oh, one more thing. There's a lumberman named Daniel Hughes who runs timber down to Baltimore. On the trip back, he picks up fugitives on his barge and brings them up to his home in Williamsport. He's a full head taller than my husband—half black, half Indian. You can't miss him. He's the tallest man I've ever seen. If you see him riding up the canal, hitch a ride with him." She squeezed our hands one last time. "Be careful. God bless." She wiped her tears on her apron and waved goodbye.

"Tillie," I whispered, "Do you know what the Missus was talkin' about? What's a towpath? Because we gonna have to find it right quick."

"Yeah, I seen it before. It runs next to the canal. The drivers walk their mules on it."

"What for?"

"Well, the mules is hooked to a big barge by a long rope. They pull that barge up the canal. Easier to move goods up a canal than up a river."

"You mean a canal be like a river?"

"Yep."

We walked into the dark. All by ourselves. With nobody to show us the way.

Chapter 19
Daniel Hughes

I hated slavers. They took me from my mama, and now they took me from the Palmers.

I hated footing it in the dark, too. Wished I had a Quaker abolitionist to stuff me in a wagon and get me to a safe place.

But I had Tillie. Now there was two of us to look out for them devil dogs and slave catchers. But could she find the canal?

The moon shone like a big yellow face, lighting our way. Star came out, too, smiling—glad to see me. I just frowned. He grinned at me anyway. I had to smile back. I had my friends—Star, Moon and Tillie.

I pointed at Star. "That there is my friend. He kept showin' me the way north when nobody else could." Tillie nodded. A smile spread across her face like she knowed all about him. She didn't say nothing. Kept walking. That was okay with me. Didn't want to wake no sleeping dogs.

We followed the road that led to town and kept an eye out. We stayed away from houses with lights in the windows, which wasn't easy. Buildings sprung up next to us like mushrooms in a meadow.

Harrisburg.

"I think I know where we are, Mose," Tillie whispered. She pointed at a big building. If I figure right—the canal is behind that store."

I stretched my neck but couldn't see nothing. We snuck down an alley next to the store.

On the other side, trees stood in front of us. Something twinkled behind them—moonlight shining on water. We done reached the canal.

Thank you, Star. Thank you, Tillie.

From what Miz Palmer said, we could follow this for a long way. I took a deep breath and let it out slow. We had a new friend to help us find our way.

Tillie hugged a tree trunk and peeked around it. "Yep. Towpath is right past this tree. We just follow this as far as we can." She looked up and down the water. "But which way do we go? We gotta get past town before daylight."

I pointed at Star. "We gotta go north, so I reckon we turn right."

The towpath was wide enough for a mule. Brush and such had been cleared away. Tillie and I could walk side-by-side. We hurried up that trail quiet as night critters.

It was still dark when we quit seeing houses. We passed cornfields. Then tree after tree crowded next to us.

"I reckon we can rest here a spell," Tillie whispered. "We got some cover." She pushed into the woods and curled up on a blanket of dried leaves.

I crawled onto a tree trunk that bent over almost to the ground and lay on it like it was a fine straw tick. I wrapped Miz Palmer's blanket around me. It sure felt good to rest my bones. I kept an ear open. "We cain't hide here in daylight, Tillie."

"I know. But I reckon I'll pass out if I don't rest a spell."

"Uh-huh." I closed my eyes.

I was dreaming about them devil dogs when I felt Tillie squeeze my arm.

"You hear that?" she said.

I sat up. Heard a belly-deep growl. A shiver grabbed hold of the back of my neck like a cold hand.

Many a time I heard bloodhounds. They never sounded like this. Three pairs of eyes flashed in the dark.

Wolves. They wanted a meal.

I pushed down the scream that wanted to bust out of me. Couldn't take no chance acting scared. I stared them down for a minute. If only I had some fatback…I could throw it past them. Maybe we could get away.

I looked at Tillie. Eyes white as china plates. She shook all over.

Wolves could smell fear.

I felt along the ground. My hand found a stick. I squeezed it tight.

Tillie saw my weapon. She picked up a big rock. Raised it up to her shoulder.

Good girl, I thought. Stuff down that fear. Get ready.

I let out a whoop like an Indian war cry. Swung my stick like a club. Tillie hollered. Threw her rock.

Snarls turned into howls. Eyes disappeared. Them wolves ran like babies scampering to their mama. I catched my breath.

Tillie grabbed my arm. "Are they gone?" she whispered.

"I dunno."

She found another big rock. I rolled up my blanket with one hand and kept a hold of my stick. We gathered our stuff and started walking. I let Tillie go ahead of me just in case the wolves came up behind us.

Bushes rustled in back of me. I spun around. Demon eyes and white teeth leaped at me. I clubbed a wolf in the nose as hard as I could. It grabbed my stick in its teeth. Tillie kicked it in the belly with a thud. It dropped my stick and ran off. I picked up my weapon and turned around, looking for another set of eyes. My heart pounded. I gasped for breath. I stood watching, ready to swing my stick. Tillie stood next to me with another rock in hand.

After awhile, my heart quit thumping. My breathing slowed. I wiped sweat off my forehead. I slung my tote over my shoulder. "Let's go."

Tillie broke off a branch to carry in case the wolves came back. She snapped off the twigs, and pushed at the dirt with it, using it as a walking stick. "We gotta hurry on. You never know who mighta heard all this goin' on. God in heaven, I hope them wolves high-tailed it for good. Lord, I know you angels been workin' overtime, but please let 'em keep watchin' over us," she whispered.

We hiked along the towpath, all the time watching for trouble. But all we heard was our own breathing and our feet busting twigs. The sky started to turn gray. It wouldn't be long before Sun's orange head would pop up behind the trees. We had to find a place to hide.

Tillie slapped my arm and stared at me with tin-plate eyes.

"Yeah, I heard it," I said. "Somebody's cussin' up a storm." They was making enough noise to wake the birds. We turned around. Tillie sucked in her breath and grabbed my arm. A big light shined in our eyes. It hung on the bow of a boat in the middle of the canal and threw light on a long boat slipping through the black water. A barge.

She shook her head. "I dunno, Mose. We may hafta go another way."

"The barge is behind us. Where we gonna go? Besides, we have to find out if that's the man Miz Palmer talked about."

"Well, we cain't figure that out in the dark, even with that big oil lamp burnin' on the bow."

She was right. And that cussing made my belly twist in a knot. Slave catchers cuss all the time. The religious folks who helped us never used the Lord's name like that. Would that half-breed cuss?

I spotted a good climbing tree where I could stay out of sight. I shimmied up it to take a good look. In the gray dawn I could make out somebody walking back and forth in front of a couple of hitched draft animals on the towpath. I guessed they was mules. As the sky turned orange I could see better. "Well, looky there."

Tillie tugged at my pant leg. "What you see?"

If my eyes wasn't playing tricks on me we was in good company.

"Mose, what's goin' on?"

I slid down the trunk. "You stay here and watch our stuff. I'm gonna get a better look."

She grabbed my sleeve as I walked away. "Mose—don't leave me here by myself."

"Don't worry. I think we found a friend."

A man with a deep voice stood on the end of the boat hollering orders.

"Look at how big that guy is," I said. He stood tall as a timber with skin dark as tree bark. His black hair fell to his shoulders, reaching past his shaggy beard.

Tillie closed her eyes. "Lord, could this be the half-breed who takes runaways upriver?" She shook her head. "I don't know, Mose. He look like a giant—just like Goliath in the Bible."

"Well, I aim to find out if he's friend or foe. One good thing. That's a black boy down the towpath fussing with them mules. Seems the lead mule is fixed on setting a spell, and there ain't nothing that boy can do about it. Just in case that boatman ain't the half-breed—you stay here. I won't let on I'm with nobody. That'll give you a chance to hide—if you have to."

"But what about you, Moses? I cain't let them take you."

I patted her hand. "Don't you fret none. I'll be okay." I took off lickety-split before she could bicker about it.

Chapter 20
Up the River

I strutted down the towpath like I owned it. If I acted like I was free, maybe that boy would think I was. He looked young enough to fool. He stood a mite taller than me but was wiry as a hickory switch. He paid me no mind as he slapped the mule's rump with his wool hat.

The tall man's voice boomed from the barge. "Robert, leave Sassafras be. She'll get up when she's got a mind to. That's okay. We'll rest here a spell." He started pulling on the towrope bringing the barge near the shore.

I froze. This ain't the way I wanted things to play out. I was supposed to talk with the boy first. If he was suspicious about me, I could get a whiff of it right quick. I could take off like lightning and leave him there fretting over his mule. Now I would have to face that giant standing on the barge. Seemed like he grew bigger and bigger the closer he floated toward us. I pressed my lips together. Pretended I was smiling. I waved.

The giant waved back. The boy, Robert, turned around to see who was behind him. He raised his eyebrows.

I guess I snuck up on him like a ghost. Wished I could disappear like one. I tugged on the front of my vest like I was somebody important. "Hello, my name is Moses." I nodded at the mule. "Guess that critter's givin' you trouble."

"Well, she's got a mind of her own." He wiped a hand on his pants and stuck it toward me. "My name is Robert."

I shook his hand. It felt warm but not firm like the doctor's or the Reverend's. The boy glanced back at the boat.

The tall man catched his eye. "Come get the feedbags. Might as well let the girls eat."

"Yes, Pa." He ran down the towpath toward the barge. The towline went slack and disappeared under the water as the long brown boat floated toward the mules. The barge looked to be only ten paces wide, but the canal was narrow, too. Two boats coming from either direction would have barely enough room to pass.

Robert pulled the line in till the boat was next to the shore then handed the rope to me. I stretched it tight while the tall man heaved the feedbags to Robert. He catched each one, swinging them to the ground in an easy rhythm like the bags was dance partners.

The giant stepped off the boat and onto the towpath as smooth as climbing out of a buggy. I wondered how a grown man could fit inside that boat—especially a man a head and a half taller than me.

He took the rope in his left hand and shook my hand with his right. His grip felt tighter than the doctor's and the Reverend's put together. He smoothed back his long frizzy hair and smiled, but his eyes cut through me. I figured he had Injun blood. Mama always said Injuns got eagle eyes. They see stuff other folks don't. I was sure he knew I was a runaway. I balled my fists and shoved them in my pockets. I hoped they wasn't shaking so bad he could see them.

"Thank you, son. Daniel Hughes, here. Who might you be?"

"My name is Moses, sir."

He wrinkled his brow into a frown and pulled on his beard. "You from around these parts?"

I dug my fingers into my palms and looked at the ground. Miz Palmer was wrong about this guy. He didn't seem too friendly to me. "No, sir. Just passin' through."

"Look at me, son."

I held my breath and looked up into them Injun eyes. They seemed to soften a bit.

"Where you headed?"

I dug at the ground with the toe of my boot. "Don't rightly know, sir. I'm lookin' for work."

He gripped my shoulder with his rough callused fingers and grinned. "Well in that case, I could use another hand till we get to Williamsport. That is, if you're heading north."

I let out the breath I was holding and pulled my hands out of my pockets. They was sweating now. I wiped them on my pants. "Thank you, sir, but I have my sister with me," I lied.

"Can she cook?"

"Why, yessir."

"Well then, go fetch her. She can help at the cook stove."

"Y-yessir!"

I turned on my heel and ran up the towpath lickety-split. In no time I had Tillie by the hand, bringing her to the barge.

She tugged at my hand and frowned. "How you know we can trust these folks, Mose?"

"Well, we got to trust somebody, and if we cain't believe Miz Palmer, then who?"

As we came near, Daniel Hughes smiled and gave Tillie a proper nod. "Pleased to make your acquaintance, miss."

"This here is my *sister*, Tillie," I told him, hoping Tillie wouldn't let on she wasn't.

"Moses says you're a mighty fine cook," he said.

Tillie lowered her eyes and gave Mr. Hughes a little curtsy. "Why thank you, sir. I'll do my best."

"As soon as the mules finish their oats, we'll push off."

Robert had slipped the feedbags on the mules while I had fetched Tillie. He walked over to the mule that wasn't so ornery. "All done, girl?" He took off her feedbag and threw it on the barge. He frowned at the other mule. "And how about you, Sassafras? How about you give us a little less sass?" He smiled at his own joke as he took off her feedbag. "I think she's ready, Pa."

Daniel Hughes hollered down into the barge's hold. "Come on up, Jeb. You can take Robert's place driving the mules."

A head popped up out of the belly of that barge. A short round man with a scraggly red beard and crooked nose climbed up a ladder and stepped onto the deck. He scowled, showing a broken front tooth. "You mean to tell me I gotta do a boy's job?"

"Quit your grumbling. There's a fresh breeze up here. You won't be cooking over a hot stove. Something to be thankful for."

Jeb stepped off the boat. He eyed Tillie up and down like a beady-eyed hawk. "I s'pose she's doin' the cookin' now."

Daniel Hughes pulled a tin of tobacco out of his coat pocket and stuck a plug in his cheek. "I suppose she is," he said without looking at Jeb. Daniel offered me the tin.

"No thank you, sir."

"Robert, help the lady onto the boat," Daniel said, glancing toward the barge."

Robert grinned. "Much obliged." He hopped onto the boat and stretched out his hand. "Come on, Miss Tillie. I'll show you around."

With an uneasy smile, she gave him her hand, put one foot on the barge, and let Robert pull her on. I hopped on like it was nothing but wobbled a bit when the boat rocked. Daniel Hughes followed.

Jeb hollered at the mules, and they started plodding up the towpath. The towrope that dangled in the water pulled tight and the barge floated up the canal.

Daniel Hughes climbed down the ladder into the bottom of that barge. "Follow me."

Tillie gave me them big eyes again. She was scared. I couldn't blame her. I wasn't gonna let on I was a mite uneasy myself. "Go on," I urged. I watched her disappear through a hatch into the hold. I gritted my teeth, grabbed the ladder and stepped onto the first rung.

Maybe Mama called me Moses, but I felt more like Jonah—dropping into the belly of a whale.

Chapter 21
Trouble for Tillie

We had to stoop over as we walked through the hold. All kinds of stuff was stacked next to us like bricks. A couple of potbelly stoves lay on their sides. Iron skillets, teakettles, and different ironware lay piled all around, too. After walking through all them goods we passed through a doorway into a room with a cook stove and table. Cots was stacked and folded up along the wall. I had to smile. These quarters was even smaller than our shack on the plantation.

Daniel Hughes sat on a stool and sprawled his long legs under the table. He looked from me to Tillie with them Injun eyes. "Are you two runaways?"

I swallowed hard and shifted from one foot to the other. Tillie stared at the floor.

"I thought so." He spread his hands on the table. "Listen, I've carried many a slave upriver. It's dangerous business for you and for me. You two will have to stay below. Can't take a chance on you being seen. Slave catchers are always on the prowl, especially since they passed the new law. We should arrive in Williamsport in a few days. Robert will take you up to the house once we get there." He looked at Tillie. "Meanwhile, you can cook for us, if you have a mind to." He pointed to a basket of eggs sitting on the floor and smiled. "I'm sure you two are hungry for breakfast."

"Yes sir," Tillie said. She picked up the eggs and set them on the table. "Y'all have any onions?"

Robert grinned big and reached into a bin next to the stove. "Yes, Miss Tillie. And here's knives and forks and such, too."

Tillie cooked us up a fine breakfast of scrambled eggs and onions in an iron skillet. Robert sliced up a loaf of bread and I slathered my piece with butter and strawberry preserves. I ain't never tasted anything so good.

Once our bellies was full, Daniel shooed us into the hold with the ironware. Tillie and I looked for a space to spread out our blankets and get comfortable.

I curled up behind a cold potbelly stove. Tillie spread her blanket out next to me. The floor wasn't soft like a straw tick, but riding in a barge floating down the canal felt a lot smoother than bouncing in a wagon bed over ruts and rocks. Seeing as how we was bone tired from fighting off wolves and walking most of the night, we fell asleep quick. I expect we slept most of the day.

I woke up smelling coffee. I stretched my legs, got on all fours, and crawled over to the doorway. A coffee pot sat on the stove spreading its perfume like a plantation lady greeting guests. I stood up and walked into the kitchen.

A creaking noise made me turn around. I looked through the kitchen doorway. Somebody opened the door to the hold. Dusty boots clomped down the ladder. It was Jeb.

Tillie sat up on one elbow. She scooted up against the stove we been sleeping next to.

Jeb crumpled his hat in his hand and stooped down next to her. She leaned away from him. He bent closer.

"Evenin', Missy." His face was inches from hers. He looked her up and down with them beady hawk eyes.

She wrinkled her nose and spit out her words. "You is drunk! Don't do nothin' you be sorry for."

Quick as lightning, he grabbed her around the middle and kissed her.

She screamed and pushed against his face. "Let me go!"

I charged through the door and shoved him. Caught him off balance. He fell to the floor. He yanked me down with him and punched me in the stomach. I socked him right in the nose.

He rolled onto his knees and stood up. Blood dripped down his shirt. He wiped his nose on his sleeve and then sneered. "Just tryin' to be friendly." He cackled till his belly shook and staggered into the kitchen.

Tillie didn't need that kinda friend. She kept twisting her skirt with her finger as she rocked back and forth next to that stove.

I shoulda knowed he would try something. I wished I never went in the kitchen. If I'd been with Tillie, he'd never have dared touch her. If he went after her again, I was gonna be right there. I wasn't letting her outta my sight.

After awhile, Daniel Hughes climbed down the ladder. "Howdy, folks." He took off his hat. "We're at a lock now, so we have to wait till the water rises before we can go forward."

We heard a whooshing sound like gushing water that seemed to come outta nowhere. I hoped that water wasn't coming in the barge.

Tillie jumped a little. She was still shook up. I wondered if she was gonna tell on Jeb.

"No need to fear," Daniel said. "Canals have locks that raise the water level so barges can float upstream. It would be impossible to move these goods upriver, especially over any falls or rapids. Canals do the job a river can't."

He went in the kitchen and poured some coffee. "What happened to you, Jeb?"

He shrugged. "Ain't nothin'. I slipped on the ladder comin' down and banged my nose."

"I'll be more careful next time." He dabbed at his nose with his sleeve. The blood had dried.

Daniel Hughes leaned in close to Jeb. He slammed his cup on the table. "You smell like whiskey! How many times do I have to tell you? No drinking on the job." Daniel reached into Jeb's vest pocket and pulled out a flask. "Go tend to the mules. Tell Robert to come down."

We watched Jeb climb up the ladder—we didn't say nothin'.

He turned to me and Tillie. "I apologize for Jeb's behavior. He's my sister's brother. I told her I'd hire him for this run up the canal." He shook his head. "He's been trouble in every job he's had. Well, this time's no different. I don't trust the man."

Tillie catched my eye. She shook her head slightly. I knowed what she was telling me. Don't say nothing about what happened. Don't make trouble.

Robert climbed down the ladder. "Listen, son, Mrs. Peterson put in an order for some pots and pans. Find me a skillet and a large pot in the cargo. I'll take it to the lock house while Jeb watches the mules. Maybe she has fresh biscuits we can buy for supper, too."

"Yes, Pa." Robert took to hunting through the cargo.

Daniel Hughes looked over at us. "You two stay put while we go through the lock. Robert will heat up some beans."

Robert handed him the pans and Daniel Hughes took them up top.

Wasn't long before Daniel came down the ladder toting a basket under one arm.

Tillie said, "My nose tells me he got them fresh biscuits."

He grinned. "You'd be right, Miss Tillie. "Chow's on."

We sat at the table like white folks at Sunday dinner, eating ham and beans with biscuits that melted in your mouth like honey.

Robert went up top and lit the lantern that hung on the bow of the barge. We rode up the

canal till way past dark. Daniel Hughes gave the word to put in for the night as he read over his paper work for the goods in the hold. Jeb and Robert tied up the barge and brought in the mules. Old Sassafras settled down in her stall behind all that ironware right quick.

Tillie and I rolled out our bedding in the hold. Robert and Jeb passed by us on their way to their cots in the kitchen. Jeb made kissing noises at Tillie. I lay down next to her. "Don't worry," I whispered. "If he makes one move, I'll take him on." I didn't fear getting kicked off the barge. If anything, Jeb might get himself kicked off.

Chapter 22
Williamsport

It was still dark when somebody touched my arm. I jerked awake. I'd been dreaming I was back on the plantation. I thought the overseer stood over me, ready to whack my hide for missing the morning work call. "S-Sorry, Buck—" I started to say.

A hand covered my mouth—but it stopped me gentle-like. I opened my eyes. Daniel Hughes stooped over me.

He put a finger to his lips and motioned for me to wake Tillie. He whispered, "We'll be docking in Williamsport in a few minutes. Jeb and I will unload the barge at daybreak, but Robert will get you to a safe place before light." He looked at me with them Injun eyes. "You gotta be careful. There's lots of folks here who don't take kindly to me helping folks get to Canada. This is a lumber town. Lots of men are hungry to make money any way they can. They'd turn you in and never look back."

I picked up my tote and twisted the drawstring around my finger. "Yessir. We'll be mindful of that. Don't want to be no trouble." I nudged Tillie. She stretched her arms and yawned.

He climbed up the ladder. "I'll let you know if it's safe to come up."

Tillie and I grabbed our stuff and waited by the ladder. I was mighty thankful that Robert was taking us to his house and we would be far away from Jeb. Wouldn't put it past Jeb to tell slave catchers our whereabouts.

Daniel Hughes looked down the hatch and whispered. "Come on."

We climbed outta that hidey-hole.

The moonlight threw gray shadows on the barge, but silver ribbons of light danced on the water. I saw some hitching posts and figured the building next to it was the livery stable. A building taller than the big house on Oakley Plantation sat so close to the canal it looked like it could fall in the water. It had an upstairs with lots of windows. A light flickered here and there. Smaller buildings huddled around it.

The mules standing on the towpath was easier to see. Sassafras flicked his tail, waiting to get out of his harness. He sure must be glad to be home and rest up awhile. I wondered if someone would rub him down good and give him oats.

Daniel Hughes rolled his eyes up to the sky. "Just our luck. There's a full moon. A perfect night for slave catchers to prowl around."

My belly knotted up just hearing him talk about them slavers.

Robert held the rope tight as Daniel Hughes hopped off the boat. He took Tillie's hand and she jumped off. I followed.

Daniel said, "Robert will get you to my place. I'll meet up with you later."

We followed Robert into town, sneaking through alleys, around rain barrels, and ducking under windows. I stooped under a window and waited for Tillie to catch up.

Something crashed and fell. A cat meowed and ran past me. I peeked around the corner. Tillie had tripped, fallen, and knocked over a crate full of vegetables. She crawled behind a rain barrel.

I held my breath. Robert and I ducked behind another crate. The window slid up. The cat leaped onto the crate we was hiding behind. A man hollered, "Get out of there, you fool cat!" He flung a rock and smacked the cat clean in its middle. It yowled, landed on all fours, and took off down the street. The window slammed shut.

The house got all quiet again. We sat there a spell and didn't say nothing. I shut my eyes, put my hand on my thumping heart, and thanked God the cat showed up to take the blame.

My throat was scratchy and I wanted to cough, but I didn't dare. Robert tapped me on the arm and pointed toward the rain barrel that Tillie hid behind. I crawled toward it, trying not to make any noise. I wished I had soft paws to pad down the alley like a cat. Tillie peeked out from her hiding place. She followed me on all fours. At the end of the alley we stood up and walked. I took her hand and squeezed it. Her fingers felt cold as ice. I couldn't say nothing to make her feel better, but I could warm that hand up a little. Maybe that would calm her down.

We passed houses and shops and a lumberyard that smelled like sawdust and sap. By and by, buildings wasn't crowded together no more. They spread out here and there. We came upon a cornfield. I hoped we was far enough away from anybody who'd come after us.

We happened upon some woods, and Robert pointed to a trail running between the trees. We walked along that until we came to a road. He pulled a roll of some kinda thin wire out of his pocket. "You stay by the trees while I string horsehair," he said. He tied the horsehair to a maple tree, strung it across the road to a tree on the other side, and pulled it tight. "I recognized Elijah Pinkney's voice back there when the cat saved our skins. Chances are, he's putting up bounty hunters at his house.

We walked past the trap. He pointed up the road. "Our house is a few miles up yonder. If they ride up this way, that horsehair will catch 'em right in the neck." He grabbed his throat and made a strangling sound. "It'll knock 'em to the ground, but it'll miss the horses."

I smiled just thinking about a slave catcher getting knocked off his horse.

We walked the rest of the way along the side of that fine dirt road. I was mighty glad to be out of the woods where I couldn't get scratched up no more. Somebody might catch sight of us in the moonlight, but Star was smiling, and I knew he could keep a secret.

Tillie rubbed her elbow and picked at her hand. "You okay?" I said.

"Just skinned up a little. Nothing to fret about," she said.

But I did fret. What if she tripped? Twisted her ankle? How far could I carry her? What if the slavers got her? Could I be a man and stand up to them and their dogs?

We rounded a corner. A house sat up on a hill like a mother hen on a nest. Wood smoke curled up from the stone chimney. We walked up a dirt path that wound up to the house.

Robert took us inside and sat us down in the kitchen. He set a log on the fire and stoked the coals till they glowed. A big kettle hung on a hook over the flames. Some kinda stew filled that pot. Just smelling it made my mouth water.

A woman tiptoed down the stairs, hugging a shawl around her shoulders. She smiled and threw her arms around us like we was kin. "So pleased to meet you both," she whispered. She rubbed Tillie's arms. "My, my, child, you're cold as a frosty mornin'." She took off her shawl and wrapped it around Tillie. "There, that's better. Robert here will take good care of you. Forgive me, but I got a sick child upstairs who needs tendin'." She climbed the stairs.

Robert dished stew onto a couple of tin plates for me and Tillie.

"Sir, you and your mom shore treat guests mighty fine," Tillie said. It was the first time I heard her talk to Robert.

He just smiled and looked her in the eye. "Only treating folks the way they're supposed to be treated."

We heard footsteps outside. Somebody knocked on the front door. Robert shooed us into the pantry and shut the pantry door. We stood in the dark. I swallowed the lump in my throat.

We heard him unbolt the big iron latch. The door whined open. "Pa, I'm glad it's you. Any trouble on the road?"

"I talked to the night watchman over at the Exchange Hotel. He said Elijah Pinkney's sniffing around town with some slave catchers. He's bound to show up here."

"I knew it," said Robert.

"I saw the trap you set. Let's hope they can't get past it."

The pantry door opened. We looked up at Daniel Hughes' smiling face. "Welcome guests. Come make yourself at home." He waved his hand toward the fire. We walked over and warmed our hands. With a twinkle in his eye he said, "I want to show you something."

He stepped into the pantry and poked his head out from behind the door. "Come on over. Now watch me. Look where I put my hand." He placed his fingers in a small groove in the wall, and slid open a secret panel.

My mouth dropped open. Tillie's eyes went round as tin plates. How could we be in that pantry and never know it had a hidey-hole? I leaned inside the secret place and ran my hand across a bench big enough for me and Tillie to sit on. I thought Daniel Hughes was right clever. I reckon he did, too, seeing as how he had a proud grin on his face.

He waved us back into the kitchen, sat down at the table, and stuffed his pipe with tobacco. We sat cross-legged on the floor with our backs to the fire and listened to him and Robert swap stories about runaways they'd brought through the hollow. Daniel blew some of that fine-smelling tobacco smoke up to the ceiling. "And I never lost one yet."

We heard horses galloping. They stopped in front of the house. Tillie and I ran into the pantry. I put my fingers in the groove just like Daniel did and opened the secret panel. As we scooted onto the bench Robert slid the board shut in front of our noses. The pantry door clicked shut.

Bam, bam, bam. "Open up, Daniel. We know you got fugitives in there."

The front door bolt rattled as it slid open.

"Why hello, Elijah," Daniel said, cool as creek water. "A bit late to come calling, isn't it?"

"From what I understand, middle of the night is your favorite time to get comp'ny." Elijah coughed. "I'm sure you don't mind if me and Blake look around. Very clever trap you set. Was that your handy work, Robert? Smart boy you got there, Daniel." His voice sizzled like lard on a skillet. "But I grabbed that wire and caught myself before I fell off my horse."

Feet stomped through the kitchen. They clumped up the stairs.

Above us, Mrs. Hughes spoke. Her voice had an edge to it. "What right you got coming into my home this time of night? You gonna scare the young 'uns."

"Well, Missus Hughes, if your husband would quit hidin' runaways, we wouldn't have to barge in like this. Seems like upstandin' citizens like yourself oughta obey the law."

The pantry door opened. I held my breath. Tillie squeezed my hand so hard I bit my lip to keep from crying. Somebody walked through the closet, taking his time. I heard his fingers slide across the shelf right above us.

Bam. He hit the secret panel. Hard. It didn't budge. We heard him spit on the floor. The pantry door slammed. Didn't hear no more shuffling around. I let out my breath. Tillie let go my hand. My head felt woozy, like when we planted all them seedlings in the hot sun and Buck didn't bring us no water.

I heard him again. "Ain't no one in here. Let's check around outside. If they ain't there, we can try the caves on the backside of the property." Feet tromped to the front door. "You're not gonna get away with this, Daniel Hughes." The door banged shut.

Daniel spoke. "Someday, Elijah, you're gonna learn not to disturb people in the middle of the night."

I leaned my head back against the wall and closed my eyes. Tillie laid her head on my shoulder. Finally, we heard the slave catchers gallop down the road.

The pantry door opened and the panel slid back. Robert poked his head in the hidey-hole. "All's clear. They're gone. Go ahead and bed down over by the fire. I'll keep an eye out, but I doubt they'll be back."

I unfolded my blanket and rolled up my tote for a pillow. Tillie snuggled next to a cat curled up by the fireplace. "Why, just look at you makin' yourself at home," I told her, grinning. She didn't smile back. Her eyes went from the door to the window.

Daniel Hughes climbed upstairs. Robert took another look out the window. "They ain't coming back," he said. "But I'll bed down here next to the fire, just in case." He took a musket off the mantel and set it next to his bedroll like it was a pillow.

Tillie scratched the kitty behind its ears and looked at me and Robert with them tin plate eyes. "Them men is comin' back for us. You cain't tell me that guy didn't know we was in there when he banged on that board. Lord knows, he's in cahoots with the devil. I believe the devil told him where we is."

I'd heard Buck say a time or two that God would help him find anybody that ran away because they was disobeying the Bible. Mama told me never to believe that. Buck was just trying to scare us so's we wouldn't leave. I figured letting the devil scare a body didn't help neither. I picked at the edge of my blanket. "Well, I believe them men are goin' to hell for sure. But I ain't so sure they know we're here."

"Well even if they don't, they could peek in them windows and see us here layin' down by the fire." She wrapped the shawl around her tight.

"You can sleep in the pantry if you like," Robert said.

"Much obliged." She picked up her bed and went in.

I got to admit, my belly got the jitters when she said they might look in the window. I bundled my stuff and followed her.

She started sniffing around the pantry shelves. I wondered what she was up to. Her eyes lit up when she found a garlic bulb. "Glory be. I got the perfect solution for them slavers." Tillie broke off a clove and rubbed it up and down the pantry door. "There," she said, all satisfied. "Ain't no devils gettin' through that."

I prayed the good Lord would keep the slave catchers and the devil away. But I put more faith in Robert's musket than in any fool garlic.

Chapter 23
Katy Jane

Noises woke me up a couple times. I thought slave catchers was after us, but it was only Mrs. Hughes tending to the sick young ’un. Once, Tillie hollered in her sleep. I put my hand on her arm and whispered, "It's okay, Tillie. We is safe." That took her out of her bad dream and she fell back asleep. But I lay there thinking how far we had come. Daniel Hughes had told us we might cross into New York by day after tomorrow. Was we close to Canada? I figured Canada had to look different than America, being it was free. Did Canada look like heaven? Maybe when we reached the border we'd walk through them pearly gates onto streets of gold.

A rooster crowed. Upstairs, folks was stirring. I peeked out the pantry door. Daniel clumped downstairs. He picked up the musket. Robert followed him out the door. Two boys and a girl trailed them outside. "Get somethin' good for dinner, Pa," the girl said.

Wasn't long before one of the boys lugged in a pile of wood and stoked the fire. The girl carried in a basket of eggs from the hen house. The other boy toted a pail of fresh milk.

Mrs. Hughes came downstairs.

I stepped out of the pantry. "Is there somethin' I can do to help?" I asked.

She smiled and shook her head. "Much obliged, Moses, but you two need to stay inside except when nature calls. Don't want bounty hunters finding you and making trouble."

"Yes, ma'am."

I poked my head just barely out the front door and spied all around. Couldn't see no slave catchers. Didn't hear no dogs. I hurried to the outhouse. Then I snuck up to the front porch and stood behind a quilt hanging out to dry. I looked down the valley and wondered where we was going next.

Daniel's house stood most of the way up the hill. Three mountains hugged the little valley. A creek ran down between two of them like a lazy snake. I blew on my fingers and stuffed my hands in my pockets. Seemed like cold weather was coming early. I walked inside.

The Hughes' clan had a passel of kids. They all stood around the table holding hands while Mrs. Hughes closed her eyes. She blessed the food, then added, "And send your heavenly angels with Moses and Tillie. Keep them safe all the way to Canada." I was much obliged for the prayer.

She set the vittles on the table. "Both of you, come here," Mrs. Hughes said to me and Tillie. "Have a seat at the table." She piled our plates with bacon and flapjacks. "You need meat on them bones to be hiking all the way to Canada."

The young 'uns took their plates and sat on the floor wherever they found a comfortable spot. Every now and then, one of them would look up and smile at us like they was used to strangers passing through.

Robert walked in the house with a grin. "My traps worked perfect." He held up a couple of fat rabbits.

Mrs. Hughes smiled right back. "We'll have a feast tonight and set these folks on their way in high style."

After breakfast she sent one of the older boys out with Robert to skin the rabbits. Everyone who wasn't toddling was shooed to the truck patch to pick vegetables.

Around lunchtime Daniel Hughes walked in. He set his musket against the wall and pulled a turkey out of his tote. "Look what I got for supper."

"Land sakes," his wife said. "Don't the Lord provide when we got company."

Daniel handed her the bird. She held it by the neck and looked it up and down like it was a fine lady. "My, my, you is a lovely bird." She held it over a pot of boiling water and dunked it quick, then hurried with it to the back door. It dripped all over that fine wood floor as she hollered. "Lemuel! Come get this turkey and pluck its feathers."

Daniel Hughes waved us over to the window. "I want to show you and Moses where you're headed tonight. That is—if Katy Jane gives you the go-ahead."

Tillie and I looked at each other. We didn't know no Katy Jane.

Daniel Hughes chuckled and pointed out the window. "See that mountain up yonder? Katy Jane lives all by herself about halfway up in a little log shanty. Years ago, she ran away from her master and has been hiding out there ever since. She'd rather risk living with bears and wildcats than white plantation folk."

Tillie rubbed her arms like she had the chills. "Ain't she afraid them critters will have her for dinner?"

"Funny thing is, they leave her alone.

"What she do up there?" I asked.

"Every night she climbs to the top of that mountain to warn runaways if slave catchers are coming. If you see two lanterns, it's safe to cross Lycoming Creek. One lantern means they're on the prowl."

I cupped my hands against the window and looked out. "How she know they're comin' if there ain't no full moon?"

Daniel grinned as he laid a hand on my shoulder. "She has spies in town. They get the word to her right quick."

Tillie twisted the corner of her apron around her finger. "Please will you show us where this creek be?"

"I'll do better'n that. If Katy says it's a go, Robert will take you till you're on the trail to Trout Run. Folks there will be expecting you. It's about ten miles. Sorry to say, I won't be here when you leave. I'm headed for the dock. We're loading lumber on the barge for a trip back down to Maryland. Jeb should have a crew filling it now."

Robert walked in. He held up the fat rabbits all shiny and dressed. "Nice, huh?"

Daniel Hughes grinned. "I'm gonna miss some fine chow. Is Lady saddled?"

"Yep, Pa. She's ready for the trip into town."

"Robert will take good care of you both." He looked over at Mrs. Hughes. "Annie, I'd like to see these two get some rest before they leave tonight."

She wiped her hands on her apron and pointed upstairs. "Tillie can lie down in Maybelle and Kathryn's bed. Robert and Lemuel's will do for Moses. Just hope we ain't too noisy for you all."

Just as she spoke, the kids tromped in with baskets of vegetables. They took them out on the back stoop and got to work snapping beans and shucking corn. "Now shoo on upstairs," she told me and Tillie. "We gonna send you off all rested up with full bellies."

We said good-bye to Daniel Hughes, watched him ride down the road, and went upstairs.

I couldn't sleep much, even though it was a fine rope bed with a straw tick. But I got to rest my bones. I opened my tote and peeked inside. It smelled like yesterday's biscuits. My writing stick didn't get much practice nowadays. I pulled out my free paper. Even though the letters was blurred, I couldn't throw it away.

By and by, Mrs. Hughes called us down for supper. She filled us up so good my body said *now* it wanted a nap. I had to tell it no—we was packing for the trip. She stuffed my tote full of cornbread, bacon, and a turkey gizzard. Tillie got the liver. We sat at the window staring at Katy Jane's mountain, waiting for the sun to go down. I closed my eyes and nodded off, sitting against the wall.

Somebody nudged me. "Take a look," Robert said. It was so dark we could barely see the mountain. But Katy Jane's lanterns shone bright as North Star on a clear night...and smiled just as big. Two lights.

Robert opened the door. The latch moaned like it was sad to see us leave. We grabbed our stuff and walked into the dark.

Chapter 24
John Montour

The moon was bright. Star wasn't so easy to see. As we walked down the hill, Robert pointed to the three mountains. In a low voice he named each one. "This one's called Scott Mountain, that one's Jacob Mountain, and over yonder is It's a Blessing Mountain. Folks say Katy Jane named 'em." He pointed to It's a Blessing Mountain. "That mountain helped many a traveler find their way when Katy Jane flashed her lantern. He walked on ahead of us down a narrow path through the woods. After a spell we came to the creek. Even in the dark I could see a winding dirt trail next to the water.

"This here is the Sheshequin Indian Trail," he said. "You can follow this all the way to Trout Run. You should get there about morning."

"Is the town right on the water?" Tillie asked.

"After the creek takes a turn to the left, you'll see a clearing with a dock. There's a road there that leads into town. Before you get into the village, you'll see a path just past an old oak tree with the initials J.A. carved in it. Go up that trail. It'll take you to Mr. and Mrs. Apker's house. If it's safe to come in, they'll have a red and white quilt hanging on the front porch." He laid a hand on my shoulder. "Good luck—and God be with you."

"Thanks," I said.

Just as Robert began the hike back up the hill, something behind us shrieked. So did Tillie.

I only heard that kinda squeal once before. A train whistle. That fearsome black monster that stole Mama must be chasing after us.

Robert Hughes heard Tillie screaming. He came running back down the hill and grabbed her hands. "My, My, you is shaking, child. Never you mind about that freight train. Just stay on the Indian path. You'll be out of its way. It can't jump the tracks and come after you."

Tillie nodded as she blinked back tears. I had told her how the train stole Mama, so she had reason to hate trains, too.

"You'll make it. We ain't lost a runaway yet, remember?" Robert said. "But you may hear that train a lot. It runs cargo from Williamsport up through Ralston."

"Yes, sir," I said. My belly eased up a little.

He walked back up the hill.

Tillie and I didn't say nothing. I led the way. The moonlight shone on the creek, making it easy to follow the path. I put one foot in front of the other and tried to forget about the train that made Mama cry.

By the time Sun poked his head through the trees, my feet was sore. More than anything I wished I could go to sleep. Even the hard ground looked like a soft bed.

We spotted the dock. Somebody stood there pulling up a fishing line. Looked like he catched something. I didn't think he saw us. "Let's cut behind him through the woods."

"What about them initials on the oak tree?" Tillie asked.

"We cain't take no chance goin' by that fisherman." I hoped we'd find the road to the safe house without that marker.

We made so much noise snapping twigs, and pushing past bushes, I feared somebody would hear us for sure. In my mind, I could hear them devil dogs snarl at me when the slave catchers almost found me in the woods. I pushed them thoughts down to my belly.

Tillie leaned against a tree, breathing hard. "I don't know Mose. This ain't easy." She closed her eyes. A tear rolled down her cheek.

I grabbed her arm. "You cain't quit now. I'm sure it ain't far."

I smelled wood smoke. "Wait here. I'm gonna look ahead to find where that smoke's comin' from."

I followed my nose till I came to a good-sized footpath. A house sat tucked in the woods at the end of that road like a white rose in the middle of a thorn bush. The quilt with the red and white squares hung on the porch rail, flapping in the breeze.

I tiptoed up to the house and took a deep breath. Should I knock?

Just as I stepped onto the porch, the door swung open. A short lady with white hair stood in the doorway. She wiped her hands on her apron and smiled. "Well, look what the Lord hath brought us."

I smiled. Quaker folk. They'd been good to me before. I pointed to the woods. "I got to go get my friend."

She nodded. "I'll wait for thee."

Tillie's eyes brightened when she saw me. She brushed leaves off her skirt. "I'm ready," she said. She looked a heap sight better since resting a spell.

"Well, we ain't goin' far." I pointed through the woods. "The Apkers live over yonder."

Mrs. Apker grinned just as big for Tillie as she did for me. She scooted us into the house. "Sit thee down and take off thy shoes." She set a washtub in front of us then grabbed a teakettle off the fire and poured hot water in the tub. She added some cold, stirred it with her finger, and smiled. "Just right. Now place thy tired feet in that nice warm water and see if that helps thee. May I ask thy names?"

"I am Moses, and this here is Tillie."

She smiled. "It is my pleasure to serve thee."

We sank our aching feet in the water. I closed my eyes and thought I would nod off right there in my chair. But the smell of cornbread and fish frying perked me up.

Mrs. Apker set two plates of food on the table. "Come have some breakfast." She bowed her head, and silently prayed. I figured that must be a Quaker way to say grace. "Enjoy your meal," she said. "I'm going to make thy beds." She walked upstairs.

Tillie and I took a big bite of fish at the same time. She rolled her eyeballs up to the ceiling. "Don't the Lord provide."

I nodded. I was ready to rest my bones.

Mrs. Apker called us upstairs. We offered to wash the dishes, but she wouldn't have none of it. "Thou hast been walking all night long. It is time for thee to rest. The back bedroom is thine, Moses, and the front one is for thee, Tillie." May the good Lord speak to thee in thy dreams."

My room had a fine wooden dresser and a chair. I sat on the bed and ran my hand across it. "Lord in heaven," I said out loud. "A feather tick." I stretched myself out, closed my eyes, and fell asleep on a mattress soft as a fluffy cloud. I swear angels was chattering not far away.

When I woke up I realized that babbling wasn't angels at all. I heard two men talking downstairs. They sounded friendly-like. A good sign.

I looked out my window. Sun had turned red and looked like it was about to touch the ground. I had slept the whole day. I rolled out of bed and cracked my door open.

"John, come in and rest a spell. My wife will get thee a cup of coffee. Molly, remember John Montour? He stopped by on his way to Elmira." I figured that voice had to be Mrs. Apker's husband.

"So good to see thee again, John. What business takes thee to Elmira?" said Mrs. Apker.

"Haven't seen my folks in a year. They're gettin' up in years. Mom took sick a few weeks ago. Could use my help at the farm."

"I am sorry to hear that. I shall pray for her. A coffee for thee, too, Jeremy?" she asked.

"Yes, thanks dear," her husband answered.

She cleared her throat. "So John...art thee riding or driving a wagon?"
"Neither. I'm gonna walk the trail and do a little trappin' on the way."

Mr. Apker spoke. "I am sorry to say, beaver hath disappeared from these woods for some time, John."

"You're right. The fur trade has moved north and west."

"Does thy father still run that fur trading business?"

"No. When the beaver ran out, he gave it up. Beaver felt for top hats is harder and harder to come by. I'm just looking for small game."

Mrs. Apker interrrupted. "John, since thy mother is half Iroquois, I suppose thou art quite knowledgeable about living off the land...." She hesitated.

"Thou hast a question, Molly?" Mr. Apker asked.

"Well, it is just that our friend has come at a most fitting time...."

"Speak up, Molly," John said.

"I have people who could possibly use thy services."

Mr. Apker cleared his throat. "Molly, did we receive guests last night?"

"Actually, early this morning, Jeremy." She paused. "John, I believe thy knowledge of Indian ways would be most helpful to our friends since they must travel all the way to Canada."

John spoke. "These guests aren't traveling by train or stagecoach?"

"No, I am afraid not," she said.

"So…if they traveled here on foot, and came by night, I assume they need protection from lawmen?"

"I know that is asking a lot, John. And I understand if that would be too much of a burden for thee…."

"I can take them to Elmira. Be glad to bless them any way I can."

"Thou art a God-fearing man, John Montour," Mrs. Apker said. "Thank you so much."

I walked downstairs. John sat at the table with the Apkers. His long black hair was pulled into a braid and hung down the middle of his back. He smiled at me through thin lips without showing no teeth. His nose hooked just a little. His small black eyes looked stern but warm, like a mama bear on the lookout. He wore white man's clothes—a linen shirt and work pants, but he had moccasins on his feet. A buckskin pack decorated with beads and feathers hung over the chair. He stood and held out his hand. I shook it. His skin was lighter than mine. If his mama had Indian blood and his daddy was a trapper, he was a half-breed. I was glad he was on our side.

"Meet John Montour," Mr. Apker said to me.

Mrs. Apker served both men their supper. "Good evening, Moses. Come eat." She stood and motioned for me to sit in her chair then set a bowl of hot stew in front of me.

Tillie came downstairs. She nodded and curtsied slightly toward John Montour.

Mrs. Apker ladled her some stew. "My, my, but thou lookest better. Sleep is God's tonic for the body."

"Thank you, ma'am, I'm grateful for the kindness you and your husband have shown Moses and me." She glanced from Mrs. Apker to Mr. Apker to John, then she smiled and took a big bite.

John looked at me and Tillie with them mama bear eyes. He knew we were runaways, but never spoke it out loud. Between mouthfuls he said, "We'll leave in a few hours—but first I'm gonna rest." He looked at Mrs. Apker.

"Oh John, please use the bed Moses slept in." She pointed upstairs.

"Thank you, ma'am," he said. He grinned big, excused himself from the table, and climbed the steps.

I looked out the window. Sun had disappeared. Just a few fingers of light waved goodbye. I watched the sky darken. Any minute now, Star would poke out his shining head to say hello.

Chapter 25
The Indian Way

Just about the time a hootie owl called out in the dark, John Montour came downstairs. Mrs. Apker packed Tillie and me dried jerky and biscuits. She threw a fresh-picked apple in the top of our packs. She offered the same to John, who nodded thank you, took the vittles, and placed them carefully in his buckskin bag. Mrs. Apker dabbed at her eye with her apron as she and her husband bid us goodbye.

John led us back down to the creek. The trail followed the water for quite a spell. Tillie and I made as much noise as ever, snapping twigs, and sometimes stumbling over rocks, but John moved smooth as a fox in the woods. As he stepped on sticks and stones, them moccasins sounded quiet as animal paws.

After we'd been walking awhile, Tillie started breathing hard. She leaned up against a tree. We stopped for a rest. I looked up in the sky. I'd only given Star a quick peek, since we been walking so fast, checking the ground and making sure we didn't trip over nothing. Now I could give him a real hello.

John put his hand on my shoulder. "You know Mama Bear?"

"Oh no, sir. Who's Mama Bear? I'm lookin' at the North Star." I pointed a finger at it. "And that there is the Drinkin' Gourd under it."

John chuckled. "What you call the Drinking Gourd, my people call the Great Bear." He pointed, too. "The four stars are the bear, and the three little stars following her are her cubs."

No wonder he had eyes like a mama bear. I figured he knew Star maybe better than I did. We was in good hands.

Tillie pushed herself up from where she sat. "I'm okay, now. We can get goin'."

We pressed on. The path turned away from the creek. Just about dawn we came upon three big trees yanked up by the roots that tumbled over one another. Musta blown over in some storm. They blocked our path.

John slapped the thick round trunk of the middle one. "Guess we'll camp here for now." He looked around. "Go ahead and lie down. I'll be right back." We were in woods so dark you couldn't see the sky, but John walked around a bit, I suppose on the lookout for critters, human or otherwise. Tillie and I unrolled our blankets and stretched out. John was back soon and seemed satisfied that we was alone. We was all bone weary and fell asleep.

I woke when I heard somebody splitting wood. John was up and had started a campfire.

I sat up on my elbows and stared at him. Didn't want to say nothing, him being a woodsman and all, but I thought the smoke might give us away.

He looked up at me and smiled. "Don't you worry, Moses. These woods are so dense, I doubt anyone will spot this fire." He added some dry pine needles for kindling. "I've never had someone come up on me in these parts. A lot of folks believe ghosts live here."

I hoped ghosts was scared of John Montour.

I watched him skin a rabbit, spear it on a stick, and set it over the fire. "Guess you set some traps when you was checkin' the woods early this mornin'."

He smiled as he turned the spit. "I reckoned we could have a proper breakfast. We can save the jerky for later."

Tillie woke up. I know she smelled that rabbit cooking. Her eyes lit up when John sliced off a piece, speared it on his hunting knife, and handed it to her.

After that fine meal, we put out the fire and rolled up our blankets. John said we should keep moving even though it was daylight. We tossed our stuff over the fallen trees. John started to climb over that mountain of logs. We followed.

Half way up, we heard a rattlesnake between the tree trunks. John moved sideways from it, across the log. The rattling stopped. He waited. Then he took another step, all careful-like. The tree trunk moved when he did. The snake sprang at his leg. He jumped off the log before it could strike. It slid back in its hole.

John put his hands on his knees and caught his breath. "Grandfather Rattlesnake, you are too slow in the shade with no sun to heat your back."

I grabbed a big stick and raised it in the air.

John put his hand in front of me. "Save your stick for walking, Moses. Never kill Grandfather. If you make war with him, he will kill you."

We walked around the logjam and through the brush. I brought my stick with me, just in case we ran into any more snakes.

After hiking most of the day, Tillie and I was bone tired, seeing as how we only slept a few hours in the early morning. John seemed to walk forever without getting weary. I could tell the woods was his friend. He looked at every tree and critter like he knowed them. About dark we came upon a lean-to. Two thick branches held up a roof made out of tree bark that slanted to the ground. He crawled inside, took out his axe, and used the blade to scrape out a family of mice, some animal bones and other trash.

Thunder rolled over our heads. He looked up with a frown. "Thought so." We hurried into the shelter just as raindrops fell. He pulled jerky out of his pack. "No fire tonight. Enjoy your dinner." He cut off a bite-sized piece and started chewing like it was a plug of tobacco, then handed me his knife. I cut a slice for me and Tillie.

John stretched out on one elbow and stared into the rain.

I heard branches rustling nearby. "Hear that?" I asked.

"Yep." He frowned and shook his head. "Might be wolves lookin' for a meal. We'll take turns keeping watch." He went out, poked around, and came back with a few leafy branches. He dragged them in front of our hidey-hole.

Maybe them wolves couldn't see us now, but I bet they could smell us. I closed my fingers around my walking stick.

Tillie sat cross-legged on her blanket and twisted a finger around a pulled thread. She looked at me. "Remember that run-in we had with wolves?"

I nodded and swallowed without meaning to.

"Well now we got one more body to help us if they come a callin'." She paused. "But if that be ghosts makin' a ruckus, ain't nothin' we can do. Didn't bring no potions to fight that." She broke off the thread, closed her eyes, and rocked back and forth. "Lord Jesus, keep us safe from whatever be out there."

We sat quiet-like and listened to the rain. I wondered if John could smell a wolf if it got close enough. I fought to keep my eyes open. I was so tired, I musta dozed off.

I woke up to the sound of twigs snapping near our lean-to. I could see John's eyes in the dark. I was pretty sure he touched a finger to his lips and help up his hand. We heard somebody cough, spit, and curse the rain. "How we supposed to find them runaways in this godforsaken place?"

I clapped a hand over my mouth. Tillie's eyes grew big. She grabbed my arm and squeezed tight. I was afraid to breathe.

"Maybe that smoke we saw yesterday was just a trapper," the voice added.

"Naw. Nobody's trapped these woods for years. I'm sure they're headed this way. A guy in Trout Run told me he saw a black boy and woman walkin' up the Indian trail when he was fishin' on the dock. That sure fits the description on the wanted poster. I promised him a few bucks once we collect the reward." He coughed again. "Let's make camp. We can start fresh tomorrow."

The voice sounded familiar.

Where had I heard it before?

"Can we find a clearing in these backwoods? Even the stars don't shine through this jungle," the first voice said.

"Quit your bellyaching."

"Yeah, well I'm wet to the bone, and chilled. That ain't good for a body in this night air."

"We can break open that bottle of whiskey when we've set up camp. That should warm us up."

They walked about a stone's throw away to bed down. We could still hear them talking. They got pretty drunk by the sound of it. When they started snoring, John rolled up his bedding and motioned for us to do the same. He pushed the branches clear of the doorway without a sound. We tiptoed out. I wished I had a pair of them fine moccasins. Couldn't even see where the stones and branches were. At least wet twigs was less likely to snap and make noise. I handed Tillie the walking stick. I figured she needed it more.

My back twitched every time I heard a hootie owl. Almost felt like that slave catcher was calling my name, but every time I looked back there was nothing there. Why did I think I knew that voice? It made my innards twist up in a knot.

I looked up but couldn't see Star. That slave catcher was right. Even the stars wouldn't come out in these woods. We followed John through the dark.

Chapter 26
Dr. Nathaniel Smith

John Montour led us for five nights. We walked through the woods and kept away from farms and towns. We never tried hiking in the daytime again—and them slave catchers never catched up with us. John taught me how to start a fire with a flint rock, how to set a snare, and how to skin a rabbit. But we didn't start no more fires till we neared the railroad worker's camp where they was laying track up to Elmira. We weren't close enough to hear voices, but we could hear them hammering. John said they was driving steel spikes. About the time they lit fires for supper, we did, too. That way the slave catchers would think our fire was in the railroad camp. I called John a fox because he was so clever. He smiled and shook his head. "Fox is my brother's name," he said. "My Indian name is He Keeps Watch." I told him his mama named him proper.

About daybreak on the fifth day we was walking alongside a creek when we catched sight of some buildings huddled together in the distance. John said that was Elmira. He pointed to a nearby farm just across the water. "See that big barn? It belongs to Dr. Nathaniel Smith. He helps freedom-loving folks like you. I'm going to take you to his place. Don't want to risk someone in town seeing you in daylight."

We walked up to the biggest barn I ever saw. He motioned us to stay back while he walked up to the door. It was open. Tillie chewed her fingernails while we waited. She handed me the walking stick. I held it like a club. I kept thinking to myself, you know you can trust John Montour. He wouldn't take you no place that isn't safe. I was kind of mad at myself for being afraid. And I hated to leave our new friend.

John came out of the barn smiling. "Dr. Smith's son, Joe, is in there milking the cow." He motioned with his arm. "Come on in."

A thin young man with dark, curly hair stood up and stuck his thumbs in his suspenders. He looked Tillie and me up and down. Tillie stared at the ground. I felt uneasy, too. I'd seen master look at me like that when he talked about selling slaves. But then Joe looked us both right in the eye like we was white folks and grinned real big. He reached out to shake my hand. "Glad to meet you folks," he said. He turned to John. "My, my, I wish all the runaways that pass through here were in as fine a shape as these two. You brought them all the way from Williamsport?"

He shook his head. "Trout Run. Took us five days."

Joe looked at us again. "My father would like to check you both to determine if you need any doctoring before we send you on." He smiled. "But you don't appear to. The last folks who passed through here were so sick and hungry, they stayed for two weeks until they got their strength back." He slapped John on the back. "You've done a good job, John Montour."

Joe dipped a cup in the milk pail and handed it to Tillie. "Would you like some?"

She nodded and gave him a little curtsy. "Thank you, sir. Much obliged."

He dipped some for me, too. It smelled fresh, tasted creamy, and felt warm going down. My belly liked that on a chilly morning.

A man poked his head in the door. "Here's my pa," Joe said.

The man raised his bushy gray eyebrows and stepped all the way in the barn. "Ah-h, guests," he said with a grin. He had the same big smile as his son. He looked us up and down like his son did too.

Joe explained to him how we got here, and his pa nodded and smiled at John Montour like he was proud of the good care he gave us. Then he wrinkled his brow. "I assume you came up to see your mother, John." He shook his head. "I've been tending her several weeks, now. Your father is helping as best he can, but can't keep up with farm chores when he's caring for your mother." He pressed his lips together. "It's brain fever." He half smiled at John. "She'll have a much better chance of recovery with you here."

I thought John's eyes looked wet, but he just blinked and nodded.

John laid a hand on my shoulder. He reached in his buckskin pack and pulled out his hunting knife. He handed it to me. "No tellin' what trouble you may run into."

My eyes musta got big as biscuits. "Oh no. I cain't take your hunting knife."

"My pa has several at the house. I won't be going without. Besides, you may need it to skin a rabbit." He smiled.

I stared at the knife in my hand. "I'm right grateful, John. Thank you." I slipped it in my tote.

John tipped his hat. "May Mama Bear watch over you on the rest of your trip."

Dr. Smith called to him as he walked out the door. "Make sure you stop at the house and get some breakfast before you go. Martha's fixing ham and biscuits. Take some for your folks. And you can borrow a horse, if you want. You'll get there faster. "

"Thanks, I will." John walked up to the house.

The cow mooed and switched her tail. Dr. Smith said, "Can't have Dolly here complaining."

Joe sat down and started milking again.

Dr. Smith took my hand and turned it over. "Field work, I'd say, from the look of these calluses. What's your name, son."

"Moses, sir. And this here is Tillie."

He smiled. "Nice to meet you both. I'll take you into town today if you're healthy enough to travel." He checked us over, asked us some questions about how we was feeling, then grinned and slapped his leg. "Let's get you up to the house for some breakfast."

We walked up to a big, two-story farmhouse. An orange cat slept in a rocking chair on the front porch. A young 'un hoed weeds in a truck patch off to the side. Mrs. Smith came to the door. She wiped sweat off her round red cheeks with her apron and smiled. "Just took a fresh batch of biscuits out of the oven." She motioned for us to come in.

I looked around for John but didn't see him. He hollered from out front. "Much obliged for the use of the horse." I looked out the window. John sat on a fine chestnut mare, waving to Dr. Smith. I ran to the door and waved back.

I wondered if I would ever see him again.

Tillie and I sat down to ham, biscuits, and gravy.

Dr. Smith nibbled on a biscuit while he walked around the house looking in corners and under furniture. "Martha, did you pack provisions for me to take to John Jones' place?"

She rolled her eyes, smiled, and nodded. "Yes dear. Joe loaded them on the floor of the carriage before he milked Dolly. So you're still making the trip to Elmira today?"

"Yes." He took a black leather satchel off a desk in the corner and set it by the

door. "I'm checking on Ettie Brown today to see if that broken arm is healing properly."

"What about Moses and Tillie?"

Tillie and I looked at each other.

"Oh, they're coming with me."

She clucked her tongue. "That will be a tight fit in a carriage made for two, Nate. And with all those bags and boxes of stuff on the floor, everybody's knees will be hitting their chins. We bought that buggy to make it easier for you to visit your patients. We didn't plan on using it like a buckboard." She sucked in her breath a little. Her eyes got round. "Oh my, them two precious ones will be in plain sight going through town. I sure don't want the sheriff catching sight of them. You can't trust him since they passed that horrible law. Amanda over at the general store said she saw a bounty hunter in town just yesterday."

Dr. Smith frowned and pulled at his beard. "You're right. We'll use the buckboard instead. Is Josh still out in the garden? Ask him to find me a canvas. I'm moving the provisions to the wagon. I'll ask Joe to unhitch Maybelle from the carriage."

Tillie and I stood at the window and watched him load the buckboard. I told Tillie about the time I rode in the wagon with the false bottom. She giggled when I told her how I tried to eat lying down. Mrs. Smith came over and put an arm around Tillie's shoulder. "Don't you worry child. My husband will get you to town safely."

Josh spread out bags of flour and corn on the wagon floor then spread a canvas over top. Dr. Smith motioned for us to come outside. Mrs. Smith gave us each a hug as she blinked away tears. We crawled into the wagon under the canvas and lay down with bags piled on either side of us. I used my rolled up blanket as a pillow. Joe tied the canvas down so it wouldn't blow away. Tillie took a couple of deep breaths and bit her lip. This seemed like a tighter space than when we hid in the hidey-hole in the pantry because the canvas fell right on our faces. I smelled salt pork. That always made my mouth water, but right now I wasn't hungry.

The buckboard started moving. I hugged my tote and thought about the things in it. I had a writing stick, and now I had me a hunting knife. That was even better than the whittling knife I'd been hoping for.

Chapter 27
Slabtown

My back banged against the wagon floor every time we hit a big rut in the road. I rolled my blanket out a little and put it under me to soften the ride. Tillie did too. After a while the road got smoother. We heard people jabbering. Wagons creaked and rumbled past us. Horses snorted like they was greeting us. I figured we musta come into Elmira.

The buckboard stopped. Dr. Smith hopped off and spoke to Maybelle. "Be a good girl and wait for me while I pick up a bag of coal." I knew them words were meant for us.

A door banged shut. A while later we heard the door open. Dr. Smith was talking to somebody. "Martha loves that coal stove I bought her." He lifted the canvas and shoved in the bag of coal. Just before he lowered the cover he gave us a quick smile. He spoke quietly to someone. "Thanks for your help, Jervis."

"It's the least I can do," he answered. "Got business in town?"

"Yep. Stopping by to look at Ettie Brown and see how that arm's doing."

"Well, just be careful," he whispered. "Folks don't take kindly to a white man doctoring folks in Slabtown."

"I appreciate your concern, Jervis, but by nature, these are dangerous times."

"How true, how true," he replied. "Did you see the latest wanted poster at the post office? A couple of bounty hunters came into town and gave it to the sheriff." He lowered his voice. "Whatever cargo you've got for Rochester you'd better ship quickly."

"Indeed...." Dr. Smith clucked at Maybelle, and we started down the road.

I held my breath and looked at Tillie. She stared at me with them tin plate eyes. We was both scared as rabbits in a trap. Were them bounty hunters the ones that followed us on the Indian trail? Are our names on that poster? Are we the cargo Jervis was talking about? And who is Rochester? Another helper taking us to Canada?

I closed my eyes and hoped that Mama was still praying for me. I prayed a little myself. About the time I whispered "amen," we came to a halt.

"Good morning," Dr. Smith said to somebody. "Or should I say good afternoon? It must be close to noon."

Another man chuckled. "Well, doctor, I guess we'll just have to invite you to eat with us."

"Don't mind if I do, but let's unload the provisions first."

"Yes sir. How about bringin' the wagon into the alley next to the church? You can drop off the goods at the side entrance."

"Thanks, John. Much obliged."

The buckboard moved forward, turned a corner, and stopped again. The canvas rolled back. Dr. Smith lifted Tillie out of the wagon. They quickly disappeared through a door. A young black man with a curly beard smiled at me. Before I could nod hello, he grabbed my hand and led me into the building.

I sat down on a bench next to Tillie. Dr. Smith put a hand on the young man's shoulder. "Moses, Tillie…I'd like you to meet John W. Jones. He's a personal friend and will be assisting you on the next leg of your trip."

"My pleasure to meet you folks. I was a runaway once myself." John picked up a broom and started to sweep the floor. Dr. Smith added, "This is the First Baptist Church. John is the caretaker."

Tillie and I looked around. I'd never been in a church before. I'd been to camp meetings in the woods on Saturday nights. Sometimes we had logs to sit on. But I usually was put on lookout. Masta knew we'd be singing about freedom. And nobody sang them songs better than my mama.

I ran my hand along the smooth dark wood. "Fanciest benches I ever saw," I said.

Tillie half smiled. She leaned over and whispered, "Church benches is called pews."

I nodded. Seemed like a funny name for benches because they didn't stink at all. They smelled warm and friendly. Which I didn't understand, since this must be a church for white folks. Maybe they was Quakers.

John grabbed a rag and wiped down a window and dusted the sill. "As soon as I finish these windows, we'll head to Ezra's next door for lunch. His wife makes a fine rabbit stew. Pastor White's comin', too." He went to the next window. "There's a pitcher of water and a basin back behind the pulpit if you want to freshen up."

"Good idea," the doctor said.

Tillie and I splashed our faces with fresh cool water. Sure felt good cleaning off sweat and dust. If we was meetin' a pastor we wanted to look respectable. I feared meetin' him a bit, since any preacher, other than Reverend Palmer, I ever saw told us to obey our masters. But I figured no abolitionist was gonna take us to that kind of preacher. At least I hoped not. We'd been able to trust the doctor so far. Sure hoped this wasn't a trap.

We walked next door to a yellow house. John knocked on the door and let himself in. "Hullo Ezra."

"Come on in." A tall black man with gray hair slowly got out of his chair and shook our hands. "Good to meet you all." He motioned us into the kitchen. An older woman who must have been his wife dipped stew into bowls and set them on the table. She smiled and bid us sit down then nodded to a black man in a gray jacket who stood next to her. "The Reverend here will say a blessing."

I closed my eyes but didn't hear the words at all. A black Reverend named White? I opened one eye halfway. He said "amen" like we was at camp meeting. He didn't pray like no white preacher. I decided black preachers sure had fine churches up north.

John, Reverend White, and Dr. Smith sat down with us. After lunch Dr. Smith handed money to me and Tillie. "Here is five dollars for both of you. You can thank Jervis Langdon for that."

The Reverend added, "Mr. Langdon provides for most of the freedom seekers in these parts, God bless him."

Dr. Smith smiled and gave money to John as well. "John has offered to take you two to Ithaca. He's renting a wagon at the livery stable."

John excused himself from the table. "I'll be back with the buckboard so we can load our cargo." He smiled at us. "Don't worry. I've made this trip before." I swallowed hard and nodded. I wished I would get used to hiding in a buckboard. But every time was like the first time.

We heard the wagon come up to the house. Dr. Smith stood up. "I'm going to help John transfer those bags from my wagon to his. Then I'll be leaving to check on Ettie Brown. May God be with you." He shook my hand, tipped his hat to Tillie, and walked outside.

Reverend White stood up. "Mind if I pray for you?"

I looked at Tillie. We nodded, folded our hands, and closed our eyes.

The Reverend slapped my head. My eyes flew open. I held my breath. His other hand was on Tillie's head.

His voice roared like a papa bear. "Heavenly Father! Rescue these children of yours from the evils of slavery. Give them angels to guide their way. Bring them safely into Canada, and let them prosper and be free." He went on some more about us getting homes and families and good jobs. He prayed for Tillie to find a husband who could support her. But when he asked the Lord to judge the slave catchers and keep them out of our way, a shiver went up my back. When he lifted his hands, I was sure them prayers musta gone straight up to heaven.

John Jones walked in the door and smiled. "Time to go to Ithaca." He said it like we was going on a Sunday picnic. I figured working at the church, he must trust the Lord.

I took Tillie's arm. We walked to the wagon like we was white folks and we been to Ithaca lots of times. I helped Tillie crawl under the canvas then scooted in next to her with the bags.

Chapter 28
Ithaca

When the wagon stopped, John pulled back the canvas. It was getting dark outside. A white church with a big steeple stood in front of us. Sun was bedding down for the night, and showing off his best colors. Red, orange, and purple fingers of light circled the church like a halo. We stepped inside.

"Wait here while I get the pastor," John said.

We sat in the dark. I ran my hand along the pew but couldn't tell if this one was as nice as the pews in the last church.

John entered with a black man carrying a lantern. When the man held it next to his face, I could see his wavy hair and straight nose. The lantern made his face glow. I thought of the times I watched the blacksmith on the plantation fire a hot poker in the forge. Simon's stern face shined bright in the light of them coals. This man had that same kind of face.

"Moses and Tillie," John said, "meet Pastor Jermain Loguen."

He gave us a thin smile. "You two will be safe in the bell tower tonight." He walked behind the pulpit and opened a door I hadn't noticed before. The door was white, like the walls, and hid in the corner. We poked our noses inside. All we could see was a skinny ladder barely big enough for a body to climb. A bell rope hung down next to it.

Pastor Loguen grinned a little bigger. "Don't worry. When you get to the top there's a platform big enough for you to sit down."

A woman came in the church carrying a basket covered with a napkin. It smelled like chicken.

Pastor Loguen tied a rope to the handle. "Moses, you climb on up there. Take the end of the rope with you. When you get settled in up top, pull up the basket."

It was my pleasure. I could smell that bird all the way up the ladder. The platform was plenty big enough for both of us. I even had room to stretch out a bit. I hauled that basket up.

Tillie followed me.

Pastor Loguen called to us, "Enjoy your meal. My wife is a good cook."

John added, "We will come for you tomorrow morning. God be with you till then."

Tillie and I lit into them drumsticks. We finished off a few biscuits with butter, too. With full bellies, we curled up on the floor and fell asleep in our new hidey-hole.

Early next morning birds woke me up. I opened my eyes and saw two pigeons sitting in the bell tower window cooing at us. I hoped they was telling us it was a fine morning.

My mama always got up in the morning and said this is the day the Lord has made, and that a good reason to rejoice. I wonder if she learned that from the birds, since they always sing at morning light.

The church bell hung right in front of us like a big cookin' kettle turned upside down. I stood up, made sure I didn't touch that bell, and looked out the window. I sucked in my breath. Lord in heaven, we was up high. I didn't pay no attention to that last night when it was dark. I looked at the floor and shook my head. We'd been sleeping right next to the edge of that platform. It's a wonder we didn't fall off.

Tillie stirred a bit in her sleep. Her legs stretched out over the edge. With a start, she woke up. "Mercy me!" she cried. She reached for the bell rope. I reached for her arm, but I was too late. She grabbed onto that rope, thinking she was gonna fall off the ledge. That bell rang in my ear louder than gunfire. Tillie let go when she understood where she was. She curled herself up in the corner like a possum playing dead. "I'm sorry, I'm sorry," she whispered.

I hunkered down and held her hand. "It's all right. We is safe." I tried hard to believe my own words. We just let the whole town know that somebody's in the church and it's not Sunday. I snuck a peek out the window. Somebody came out of the house across the street and ran toward us. I ducked down before I could tell who it was. The church door opened. We heard footsteps. The bell tower door opened.

"You all right up there?" It sounded like the pastor.

I peeked over the edge of the platform. "Yes, sir. Sorry sir."

"Well come on down. We need to move you two while I think of an excuse why we rang that bell."

We climbed down and hurried across the street into his house. Mrs. Longruen shooed us into the cellar while John Jones hitched up the buckboard. John called us upstairs. "Hurry up and get in the wagon. We're leaving earlier than I planned."

We were under that canvas in no time. John trotted the horse a bit faster than usual. My heart was pounding faster than usual, too. Tillie looked afraid and mad at the same time. I knew she would blame herself if we got caught. I took her hand. "Don't go frettin' about this. We gonna be all right." I sure hoped so.

Chapter 29
George Johnson

Wasn't too long before we stopped. John got out of the wagon. We heard him walk into a building. Folks came out of the place. One of them said, "Wasn't expectin' you this early, John. But it's just as well. The shop won't open till ten. I can get cargo put away before I get customers."

The canvas rolled back. Another black man stood next to John, smiling all friendly-like. "This here is George Johnson. He's a barber." John whispered as he gave Tillie a hand. "Go between the buildings. We'll let you in the back door."

George led the way and snuck us in. We walked upstairs into some living quarters and all the way to the bedroom. He opened a tall brown wardrobe. "If you hear somebody comin', climb in here." He turned to John. "Did I hear the bell ring over at the A.M.E. church?" John looked at the floor and shook his head. "Just a little mishap. We got over here quick in case some fool slavery sympathizer went to check it out."

George frowned and rubbed his gray beard. "It's a good thing. Bounty hunters rode into town last night. They're staying at the hotel." He smiled. "Well, if they're looking for these two, maybe pokin' around the church will keep them off their trail."

John nodded and sighed. "Thanks, George. Can you take it from here? If I leave now I can be in Elmira before dark."

"My pleasure."

John shook my hand. "You are a brave lad." He took Tillie's hands in both of his and spoke to her gently. "George here will take good care of you. God bless." We thanked John for his help and he walked out to the buckboard.

Tillie bit her lip. I knew she was still scared she'd messed up our getaway.

George opened a black wooden trunk filled with clothes. "I want you to pick out a nice dress," he said to Tillie. We're gonna make you look like a fine maidservant for a high society lady.

Tillie blinked back tears. "Thank you," she whispered.

"When you've picked out your clothes, go see my wife. She's running you a bath right now. No one will suspect you're a runaway all cleaned up in a new dress." Tillie's face brightened like North Star. She had something to keep her mind off that blamed church bell.

George looked at me. "Moses, come on. I'm giving you a haircut."

He led me downstairs to a barbershop. He patted a special chair with a high seat and motioned for me to sit down. The black leather seat felt soft. I rested my feet on a special stool. A real mirror hung on the wall, and I got to watch him cut my hair. It had grown long since I ran away. He cut it pretty short, and also shaved a few whiskers off my chin.

George grinned. "My, my, don't you look fine. And you ain't even had your bath yet."

I stared in the mirror for a long time. I hardly ever got to look at myself. It felt like Mama was watching me. I had her eyes. With my short hair and new clothes, I was gonna look every bit like a free man. Mama's dream was coming true.

George patted me on the shoulder. "Upstairs with you, young man. We gonna finish your transformation." I figured a transformation was a good thing.

George helped me pick out a new shirt and trousers. He pulled off my boots and lent a hand cleaning them. I rubbed them with a soft cloth till they shined.

Once Tillie and I was dressed in our fineries, we stood in front of the Johnsons. I checked to make sure all my buttons was buttoned on my new white shirt. I tugged on my vest, which seemed a little tight to me, but George said that was the way folks wore them. Over the top of all that I wore a jacket, which I figured would keep me warm now that the weather was getting cooler. Tillie smoothed out the light blue dress she wore and fiddled with the white shawl she wore around her shoulders. "Mm—mm," Miz Johnson said, "If you two don't look good enough to wait on a king and queen."

Tillie smiled and curtsied. "Why ma'am, it would be my pleasure to help you dress in your gown for the ball this evenin'."

Miz Johnson laughed till tears ran down her round cheeks. "Why, you gonna make a fine lady's maid." She tilted Tillie's chin up with her finger. "Hold your head up, girl. You got every reason to be proud. You're a fine woman."

Tillie wiped away a tear. "Thank you ma'am."

We stayed at the Johnson's that night. George woke us out of bed before the birds was up. We dressed and climbed in a carriage that looked just like the one Dr. Smith had. We sat on that black leather seat before God and everybody like we was respectable folks and rode off.

Sun peeked from behind the mountains to check on us. We weren't far past the barbershop when George handed me the reins. "Nobody's up and around yet. This is a good time to get a lesson on how to drive a carriage. If you're gonna look like a gentleman's footman, you'd better know how to be one. And Sally May is an easy goer."

Tillie giggled when she saw the surprised look on my face.

"Feed the reins through your fingers," George said. "That's right. Bring 'em from your hand up through your thumb."

I pulled up on the reins and Sally May stopped.

George put his hands over mine. "Don't hold 'em so tight. Give her a little slack. You want to feel the horse through the reins, and you want the horse to feel you." George flapped the reins and Sally May started to trot. "We want to turn that corner up there. Just pull the reins to the left a bit."

We got to the corner, and I tugged her toward the left. She made the corner perfect. I smiled at George.

He smiled back. "You're gettin' the hang of this. Now stop next to that boat dock."

"Boat dock?" I stared at a whopping big lake. I looked out over the water and couldn't see the end. It seemed to just drop off the earth.

I pulled back on the reins. "Whoa, Sally May." She halted right next to a gangway that led to the biggest boat I ever laid eyes on. "Excuse me, Mr. Johnson…where are we? You never said nothin' about no boat."

He smiled. "I reckon I didn't. This here is Cayuga Lake you'll be crossing."

"Pardon me, I don't mean to be unthankful or nothin', but I cain't see the end of it."

"It's forty miles long, son."

He pointed to the boat. "And this here is The Simeon Dewitt, finest steamboat on the lake. She will have you at the Cayuga Bridge by one o'clock this afternoon. There was no sense worrying you till I knew this was the plan."

I swallowed hard. This wasn't no canal boat. She looked like a sea monster. She had two decks with white rails like rows of teeth. A big black smokestack reached up to the sky blowing smoke like she was puffing a cigar. A round box that reached up past the second deck hugged the side of the boat. It had letters on it painted blue. I could read an "S" and a "D." I knew it must be the boat's name. Men hauled wood up the gangway and piled it on the deck. Other workers carried boxes, crates, and the like. Men, women and children stood around waiting to get on.

"Don't worry," George said. The captain knows us. I send him folks every now and again." He looked around to make sure nobody else could hear. "Look for my cousin who works at the train depot when you get off. He can put you on a train to Rochester. Then you just have to board another steamer across Lake Ontario and you're in Canada."

Tillie and I stared at each other. We was getting close. And now I knew that Rochester was a place, not a person. When we got there we would almost be home.

"Well don't just sit there, come on," he said. We got out of the carriage and followed him like two ducklings following their mama. He walked up to a bearded man wearing a cap. George tipped his hat. "Hello, Captain Buckbee, so good to see you again." He handed him some money. "Mayor Johnson sends his regards." George put a hand on my shoulder. "Let me introduce the mayor's servants, Moses and Tillie. He is sending them to Seneca Falls to help out his sister. Her children have fallen ill and she could use the help."

Captain Buckbee grinned. He had a mustache and beard that made his chubby red face look even fatter. "So good to see you again, George. I appreciate your business."

The captain shook my hand firmly and smiled. "Glad to meet you both. Come on board. Go up front by the boiler room. There are places to sit by the cargo."

We thanked George, said goodbye, and followed the captain up the gangway.

Chapter 30
A Close Call

We figured out right quick where the boiler room was, because it felt hot as a steaming pot when you got next to it. Men went back and forth through the door, carrying loads of wood. I couldn't see them feeding the fire, but I saw black smoke come out of the smokestack. The whistle blasted, and the boat rumbled forward. It sounded a lot like a train whistle. Gave me the shivers.

Tillie grabbed my arm and pulled me next to a crate of squawking chickens. "What's the matter with you, Mose? You cain't just stare off into space. We gotta keep an eye out for trouble. Most of the white folk are goin' to the upper deck. We gotta lay low and don't cause no ruckus."

She was right. We wasn't used to being out where anybody could see us. We crawled behind a big tub and started watching people. I felt more at ease behind the boiler room around the barrels and bags of stuff.

I heard water splashing. It came from the big round box. Then I knew. A wheel inside that box was moving us through the water. Sounded just like the wheel at the flourmill scooping water.

The captain walked by. He pointed at some cargo and told a worker. "Stow whatever will fit in the hold." The man opened a hatch on the floor near us and climbed in. Another man passed him sacks of flour and such. I didn't think the tub and the chickens would fit.

Suddenly, Tillie dug her fingernails into my arm. Hard. I almost came to tears. She crouched behind the tub and pointed. A man with a chipped tooth and crooked nose stood not far away. A gun and holster was strapped around his middle. He turned his back to us and lit a cigar. His gun belt was filled with bullets.

A cold chill ran up my back even though I was sitting next to that hot boiler.

It was Jeb, the hired hand on the canal boat that kissed Tillie.

He said to a man next to him, "Let's talk to the captain." They walked out of our sight.

I pressed my hands against my forehead to keep from shaking. It all made sense now. The slave catcher's voice I heard when we was on the trail with John Montour. I'd been trying to figure out where I'd heard it before. It was Jeb. He'd been following us all this time.

Tillie looked at me and whispered, "We got to hide someplace."

I kept my eye on the men loading cargo in the hold. They closed the hatch and walked away.

I nodded at Tillie. She knew what I was thinking. We waited till nobody was around. I told myself, *You got to get in that hide-hole or you and Tillie got no chance.* I crawled to the hatch expecting a bullet to hit me. I opened it and motioned for Tillie to go in.

She froze.

I looked around for Jeb. If she didn't move soon we was both dead. I whispered, "Come on!"

She skittered down that hole faster than a rabbit. I slid in right behind her and pulled the hatch over us.

I tried to catch my breath. The air felt hot and stuffy like I was breathing through cotton. Sweat dripped into my eyes. Was I gonna die getting smothered in a hole? We tried to crawl around and get comfortable. Bags and boxes kept getting in our way. There wasn't room for a body to stand. Underneath that boiler it was darker than a starless night and hotter than a tobacco field in August. But the worst thing was the noise. Steam hissed like a mad cat. Metal clanked and scraped till I thought the boat might shake apart. Men yelled to each other over that racket.

"More wood for the fire."

"Ash bin's filling up. Go dump it."

"Add more water to the boiler."

I felt Tillie shaking next to me. Right now I wished I was back on the plantation. I'd rather get fifty lashes than hear them horrible sounds.

Tillie quit moving. She musta passed out. Did that cotton air smother the life out of her? I poked her arm. She lay there like a rag doll. I bit my fist. Oh God, please don't let her die. I put my hand up to her nose. She was still breathing. I sighed and fell back on a gunnysack. "Oh, Lord, if you get me and Tillie out of here, I'll do whatever you want."

I started to wonder if I was supposed to go back. Maybe them white preachers was right. Maybe God created black folks to serve whites. Maybe that's what God wanted. I thought about turning myself in, but I couldn't do that to Tillie.

It seemed like we'd been in this hellhole forever when a bell rang.

"No more wood. We're getting ready to land."

The hissing and clanking stopped. My ears kept ringing.

Tillie grabbed my arm. I squeezed her hand tight and wouldn't let go.

Thank you, Jesus. She ain't dead.

Above us, folks talked and walked. I didn't dare open the hatch. I wondered who would.

The chatter died down. "That's funny, the hold ain't locked," somebody said above us. The hatch opened. A man lowered himself into the hold. "Well, for the love…," he said then hoisted himself outta the hole. "Cap'n. You gotta see this. I think this here is some of your cargo."

The captain bent down and peeked into the hold. "Well, my Lord. I wondered what happened to you two." He looked over his shoulder then gave me his hand. "Come on. The men who were looking for you are gone."

"How'd you know?" I asked.

The man who opened the hatch lifted Tillie out.

"They asked me about you. Had wanted posters. I told them I hadn't seen you," the captain said. He looked around again. "Frank here will take you over to the train depot after the crowd clears out. We'll sneak you in the back where they store the freight. Just act like you're free and you belong here."

"Yes, sir. Thank you sir," I said.

Tillie nodded. She tucked her hair back under her head wrap and smoothed out her skirt. We hid behind the boiler till everybody was gone. I told her, "Remember, you a lady's maid and got sick young 'uns to care for in Seneca Falls." She smiled and held her head up high. We walked down the gangway with Frank.

Chapter 31
Train Ride

Frank did a good job leading us past all the folks. Some was meeting friends and relatives. Others stood in line at what Frank said was the railroad ticket office. They was all so busy with their own business they didn't see us sneak into the back room.

Frank patted a big trunk. "Come sit down. I'll let Sam know you're here. He'll put you in the baggage car, no doubt." He smiled and tipped his hat. "I have to get back to the ship. We leave for Ithaca soon. You're almost there. Have a safe trip to Canada."

"Thank you. And thank the captain for us," I said. We waved goodbye.

Tillie smoothed out her dress some more and rearranged her shawl. She unrolled a corner of her blanket and wiped off her face. "It ain't easy lookin' respectable after bein' in that hole."

I had to say I was mighty glad we was out of there.

Before long a black man in a white shirt, gray vest, and jacket came in. He raised his eyebrows. "Ooh, don't you two look mighty fine. Been to see my cousin George?"

We nodded.

"Well givin' folks respectable clothes is one of his specialties." He shook my hand and nodded at Tillie. "Hello, I'm Sam."

Tillie stared at him with her mouth open. "Well, thank you, sir. That's mighty kind of you. But the truth is we is tired. Ain't had nothin' to eat or drink since dawn this mornin'." Then she made herself smile and curtsied. "Sorry, sir. Travelin' in tight places can make a body outta sorts. I'm Tillie, and this here is Moses."

"Why, yes. Of course, you're thirsty. Let me see what I can do. There's a pump down the road. I'll be right back."

Sam returned in no time with a bucket of water, a drinking gourd, and a couple of apples. "Sorry I don't have more," he said.

Tillie shook her head. "Don't be sorry. We is thankful to the Lord and grateful to you for what you brought. We know you takin' a big risk helpin' us."

Sam nodded. "Well, now the trick is getting you in the baggage car without being seen." He looked outside. "Everybody's on board, and they're loading the last of the bags." He motioned for us to stand up. "Tillie, could you grab your belongings, and Moses' stuff, too? I have a plan. Moses, how about you lift the other end of this trunk. We'll walk out there like we're loading freight, then you two hop on."

I swallowed hard. "Yes, sir."

Tillie grabbed our totes and bedrolls. Sam and I picked up the trunk. We walked outside.

Folks was waving goodbye to their families and friends. They didn't seem to pay us no mind. The baggage car door stood wide open. I hopped onto the car and pulled the trunk in as Sam lifted it from behind. His eyes ran up and down the track as he lifted Tillie into the car. "Good job, Moses." He walked back to the station with hands in his pockets and a smile on his face. I heard him tell the conductor, "Freight's all loaded, sir."

We tiptoed to the corner as far away from the door as we could get. It still stood open. Besides trunks and such there was bags of grain and farm equipment. I recognized a horse-drawn plow but didn't know what the other metal stuff was.

"All aboard for Geneva, Canandaigua, and Rochester."

The door slid shut. We heard the bolt latch from the outside. The whistle blasted. The train jerked forward.

I lost my balance and fell on the ground. A big knothole the size of my fist had been knocked out of a plank in the floor. I stared down at the track underneath us. As the train picked up speed, the track turned into a blur. I ain't never rode on something that went so fast.

I looked up at Tillie but couldn't see her face. There wasn't no windows. She sat down next to me and took my arm. Her fingers felt cold. I could see them now. My eyes had got used to the dark.

"Do you still have the covers?" I asked.

"Mm—hm." She wrapped herself up.

"We almost there, Mose." She rolled out my blanket and put it around my shoulders. "We may be free as soon as tomorrow."

"Yeah, maybe." I thought about the promise I made to God. Did He want me free? I know Mama did. And He and Mama was in cahoots with one another. Where was Mama now? Where did the train she rode take her? I hoped she knowed I was riding a freedom train.

I leaned against the wall and closed my eyes. The train rocked back and forth and sang a clickety clack lullaby. It put me to sleep.

Steam hissing woke me up. "Geneva," the conductor called. The train stopped. The door opened. Somebody threw on some bags. The train chugged forward. I hugged my legs and kept my eyes open.

"Canandaigua." More bags came on. Somebody hopped in the car and loaded freight. We hid behind some bags of corn. I held my breath. They jumped off without paying us no mind. The door slid shut. I took a deep breath and squeezed Tillie's hand.

"Last stop, Rochester, New York." The train pulled out of Canandaigua. I stared at the

knot in the floor. We was racing to Canada.

Chapter 32
Rochester

Steam hissed as the train chugged to a stop. It seemed like it took twice as long to get to Rochester as it took to get to them other cities. But I could still see light through the knothole, so I knew it was still daytime.

Tillie nudged me. "I cain't believe we come this far so fast. A boat in the mornin', and a train in the afternoon. My, my." She took my hand and squeezed it with icy fingers. "But Mose…how we gonna get off without bein' seen?"

I'd been thinking about that. Would we get this far just to have Jeb snatch us off the train? Somebody would be unloading bags soon. "Just pray that whoever hops on this car is a friend." We crawled behind the big trunk.

The door slid open. A black man in a cap and jacket climbed on. He grabbed a bag and threw it to somebody on the ground. "William, come up and hep me wit this trunk." He grabbed a handle, started to drag it, then dropped the handle. He saw me. His mouth hung open like he saw a ghost. My eyes felt like they was popping out of my head, I was so scared. He stooped next to the trunk and pushed it with both hands. "Don't bother, William. I got it to the door." He hopped off and the two of them lifted it to the ground. He climbed back on and passed the rest of the bags to William. "See to it that all the passengers get their luggage," he said to him. "We'll unload the farm equipment after that."

Me and Tillie sat huddled together. He knelt down and whispered, "I'll watch the door and let you know when folks is gone, or at least ain't lookin' this way. Get over to the print shop on Buffalo Street. Frederick Douglass runs that place, and he's the head stationmaster here." He took another quick look out the door. "It's across from the Reynolds Arcade. That's a big buildin' with lots of stores in it. Somebody at the print shop will take you in. Good luck." He started to leave but stopped. "We need a signal, so's I don't call no attention to you gettin' off. When it's safe to go, I'll cough, okay?" We both nodded. The kind brother whose name we didn't know hopped down.

Sweat dripped down my head and stung my eyes. I wiped it off with my sleeve. Took Tillie's hand. She shook like a rabbit in a snare.

We heard him cough. I tiptoed to the door and peeked out. People walked to our right toting bags. I paid them no mind and jumped off.

Tillie stood in the door, stiff as ice on a creek. "Come on," I whispered. I picked her up by the waist and stood her on the ground like one of Miz Oakley's china statues. The man pointed left. "Head up yonder."

I grabbed Tillie by the hand and pulled her up the street. When we were a block from the train, she came to her senses and started running without my help.

I wondered how we was gonna find Buffalo Street. Tillie pointed to a signpost like she was reading my mind. "Them is street signs. Look for one that starts with a 'B,' Mose."

People stared at us funny when we ran, so we slowed down and smoothed out our clothes. Acting like respectable folks who belonged here was a better plan.

The sun dipped low between the buildings. It would be dark soon.

Tillie pointed to a street sign. "Here it is."

We looked up and down the road. People stood around a big building. It was the tallest, widest I ever saw, with lots of windows. Them windows shined with the light of the late afternoon sun. They looked like wolf eyes watching the street.

"That's gotta be the Reynolds Building," Tillie said. We walked that way.

A building just as tall but half as wide stood across from it. A newspaper was tacked to the front door. Tillie and I looked at each other. Could this be the print shop? We walked up the front steps. The paper had lots of little words on it, but two big words was at the top, and a picture was between them. She ran her fingers across the big letters. "North Star," she read. The picture showed a black man walking up a road in the dark all alone. He looked up at a star.

Gave me chills, just looking at that picture. That man was telling my story.

We knocked on the door.

A white woman answered. Her eyes widened. She threw her arms around us and gathered us inside like a mother hen guarding her chicks. She shut the door.

She smiled and patted her light brown hair pinned up all like Miz's. If it wasn't for her shiny black frock and white lace collar, I woulda swore she looked like a plantation lady. She pointed downstairs. "This way." She floated down the steps like a black swan.

The cellar seemed a bit musty, but mostly smelled of something that stung my nose. I guessed it was ink, or some kind of cleaner. A black man in a dress shirt, vest, and jacket sat at a desk in the middle of the small room. He paid no mind to the machine in front of him that looked like a giant box with a hinged lid, or the young white man with an ink-stained apron who laid a sheet of blank paper on it. The man at the desk wrinkled his brow, dipped his pen in an inkwell, and wrote.

A young girl looked over his shoulder, holding a stack of newspapers. "Pa, we have company."

"Yes, Frederick, we have guests." The swan lady said it like we was a prince and princess.

He raised his eyebrows and pushed his chair back. He rose up like a black bear on hind legs. Shook my hand with a firm grip and shook Tillie's too. He smiled. "How are you? I'm Frederick Douglass. He nodded toward the swan lady and the others. "This is Julia Griffiths, my manager. My daughter, Rosetta, and one of my helpers, Joseph Post."

Tillie curtsied. "Pleased to meet you. I'm Tillie."

I nodded with my mouth hanging open.

Tillie stared at me. I knowed she expected me to introduce myself proper, but I couldn't spit out a word.

"The cat's got his tongue, but this here is Moses," she said.

Frederick Douglass looked at me with mama bear eyes, just like John Montour did. But John spoke quiet as a fox. I figured this man could roar like a bear, and his enemies would get out of the way. I knowed nothing was gonna scare him.

"How'd you two get here?"

Tillie cleared her throat. "The train. We hid in the baggage car. And this morning we took a steamboat up Cayuga Lake."

He nodded. "Have you eaten?"

"Just a few apples, sir."

"We'll see you get something."

He turned to Joseph. "Does your dad have room for two guests tonight?"

Joseph wiped his hands on his apron. "I'm sure of it, sir. It's been a week since we had folks come through. I think Ma is going to market to pick up provisions."

Mr. Douglass clapped his hands together. "Wonderful. Rosetta. Would you run up to the drugstore and let Mr. Post know they can expect company at their house tonight? And stop by the bakery for a loaf of bread."

"Yes, Pa."

"Julia, could you check if any steamships leave for Ontario tomorrow, and do we know the captains?"

She nodded.

After they left, he sat back down and pointed to a couple of chairs. "Please sit down." He folded his hands in his lap. "How old you are, son?"

I smoothed out my vest and stood straighter. "Maybe twelve, sir?"

"That's about how old I was when I first learned to read. Do you know how?"

Tillie cleared her throat. "I been teachin' him his numbers and letters."

I nodded. "I can write my name."

"Good. That's a great start." He looked at Tillie. "So who taught you to read, young lady?"

"Miz Palmer, sir. She and the Reveren' kept me most of three years before sendin' me on to Canada."

He frowned. "Yes, the Fugitive Slave Act has changed everything unfortunately. But I'm very impressed with your schooling. Every young lady should be educated. Don't let anyone tell you otherwise."

She curtsied again. "Thank you, sir. That's what Miz Palmer said when she taught me."

"Smart lady," he said. "Do either of you have any questions for me?"

I sat down across from him and folded my hands, too. What could I ask him? How did a black man get so important he could run his own newspaper? Did the slave catchers still try to come after him? I had so many questions. I didn't know where to start.

He handed us each a copy of the paper. "Tillie can read this to you. This paper helps people know how wrong slavery is. Someday you'll read this by yourself, Moses."

Tillie started fiddling with her head wrap. "Why yes. Miz Palmer used to read us freedom papers by them 'bolitionists, sir. Moses, here, even wrote hisself a freedom paper before we left."

I closed my eyes and sank down in my chair. An important man like Mr. Douglass prob'ly thought that was a fool notion for a boy who cain't write but a few words. Why'd she tell him?

When I looked up, Frederick Douglass was staring at me.

"I would like to read your freedom paper, Moses."

"Sorry, sir, but it ain't here. It got hid away in Miz Palmer's cellar."

I was kinda glad now that I snuck it in that hidey-hole. There's something scary about putting your heart on a paper where everybody can see it. Especially somebody as important as Mr. Douglass.

"Can you tell me what you wrote?"

The words stuck in my throat.

Tillie poked me. "Go on, Mose."

I looked down at Mr. Douglass's paper and that fine picture of the black man following the North Star. "Well, sir…it was about how I'm free now and I can learn to read and write and have my own job and make my own money."

"Excellent. So you're a writer, too, eh?"

"Not yet, sir."

He took my newspaper and laid it on the desk. He held my hands in his giant fingers like he was God himself.

His voice rumbled like thunder breaking over mountains. "What is possible for me is possible for you. Believe in yourself and take advantage of every opportunity." He folded my paper and handed it back to me. "Moses, someday you may write an article for this paper."

I blinked. "Th-Thank you, s-sir." I always knowed someday I would learn to read and write—but for a newspaper? One that helped black folks get free? Mama always said I was gonna help slaves.

I was gonna have to take the lid off my box of dreams.

Chapter 33
A Wild Buggy Ride

The door flew open. Rosetta rushed in, panting like a racehorse. "Papa, Jacob Morris over at the barber shop heard tell there's slave catchers in town."

Tillie slapped both hands over her mouth.

I grabbed the sides of my chair.

Frederick Douglass stood up. "Where are they now?"

"One of his customers said two men with guns just checked in at the hotel."

"Thank you, Rosetta. Take Moses and Tillie up to Mr. Martin's office on the first floor and hide them there. My business will be the first place they'll come looking." He frowned as he straightened papers on the desk. "What did Mr. Post say?"

"He sent word to his wife to bring the buggy by. They'll pick them up later."

"Good. It will be dark in a few hours. Let's take them then." He stroked his beard and looked at Joseph. "Will they be safe at your parents?"

Joseph's eyes darted from Mr. Douglass to me to Tillie. "Wouldn't be the first time bounty hunters sniffed around our place." He forced a smile. "But we haven't lost one yet."

Rosetta grabbed a key off a hook and led us upstairs. She unlocked a door and let us in. "Mr. Martin is away, but he lets us use his place for such occasions."

She handed Tillie a loaf of white bread. "Glad I got to the bakery. Leastways you'll have full bellies before you go." She made a tight-lipped smile and shut the door. The key clicked as she turned it in the lock. Her shoes clacked as she rushed downstairs.

We was all alone. I felt like a baby left in the hot sun while his mama picked tobacco. I told myself, Moses, you got to get your mind off of what bad stuff might happen. Tillie and I got a whole loaf of bread to fill our bellies. Think about that.

We sat on the floor next to a desk piled with papers and pulled apart that fine bread. White bread sure melts in your mouth.

Every bit of daylight was gone when the key turned in the lock. Mr. Douglass stood in the doorway holding a lantern. "Joseph is ready." He motioned us outside. "Quiet now."

Frederick Douglass took Tillie's hand as she stepped up into the buggy. I grabbed the rail and pulled myself on. The carriage lantern shed light on the shiny black horse and the soft seat with the backrest. This buggy looked like the one Dr. Smith owned. Lightweight, no storage, and a leather cover that folded behind us like a fan. Mr. Douglass tipped his hat and smiled. His eyes shined like stars. "Godspeed and safe travel for you both."

Them words stirred me like rain from heaven. "Thank you, sir." I gripped the edge of the bench and hung onto his words. I hoped God was speeding us to freedom.

Joseph flicked the reins. We pulled away from the print shop.

Tonight the air nipped at my fingers a little bit more. I was thankful for my new vest and jacket. I buttoned up. I was glad we didn't look like runaways. We rounded a corner. Shops and homes was fewer and farther between.

Joseph pointed to a two-story house with lights in the windows. "Almost home," he whispered.

Bang! A gun fired. Tillie screamed.

The horse neighed and danced sideways. The buggy shook so bad we almost fell out. Joseph pulled up on the reins. "Whoa! Easy, Shadow."

A black hand grabbed the bridle and steadied her. A white hand pointed a pistol an arm's length from Joseph's face.

Tillie dug her nails into my arm and hid her face behind my shoulder. I didn't dare scream. I wanted to run, but I couldn't leave Tillie.

"Scared you, huh?" The white man croaked like a toad. He pointed the gun in the air and fired off another shot. He wheezed and laughed. "Wouldn't want to hurt the merchandise."

I knew that voice. He moved into the lamplight. Crooked nose. Broken tooth. My heart dropped to my belly. It was Jeb.

He said to Joseph, "Why son, you realize you harborin' fugitives? You got law trouble." He smiled through a plug of brown chaw. His eyes danced like demons. He waved the gun under Joseph's nose. "Just hand these darkies over to me and Aaron, here, and we won't say nothin' to the sheriff. No sense spendin' six months in jail." He planted his foot on a spoke and leaned into the buggy. "I'm doin' you a favor, son." He grinned and spit tobacco on Joseph's shoe.

Joseph stiffened. Clenched and unclenched a fist. He set the reins on the seat and slid them next to me. He looked at me quick as he slid his hand back to his side. I knowed what his eyes was saying. He wanted me to run off with this buggy. I snuck my hand onto the reins.

He turned to Jeb. "Now see here. These are free people. They work for my pa."

I kept my hand on the seat like I wasn't holding nothing, but I knowed that leather strap hid under my fingers. Joseph stared at me again as he climbed down. His eyes said watch me. He walked away from the buggy.

Jeb took his foot off the spoke and followed him. I breathed out slow and squeezed the reins.

Joseph said, "They have a right to be here. Tillie cooks and cleans for my ma. Moses makes deliveries for the drugstore."

Jeb spit on the ground. "Oh yeah? Well we got papers that say otherwise."

The man holding the bridle stepped toward me.

I saw his face in the lamplight. Wide flat nose. Thick lips. A scar across his cheek. He was black.

How could you turn on your own kind? Only if your heart was black. Or maybe he didn't have a heart. He was worse than Bitsy back at the plantation. She always told on folks that planned to run away. But she never went looking for them. My face burned so hot I thought I might catch fire. I wanted to spit in his face.

"What's going on here?" A man stood on the front porch holding a lantern.

"Pa, these men are trying to take our friends," Joseph said.

Joseph's pa walked over and shined the light in Jeb's face. "Put the gun down, sir."

Jeb sneered. "Show him the ad, Aaron."

Aaron let go of the bridle.

I held my breath. Slid the reins onto my lap. Closed my other hand around the strap. I tried to breathe slow, but my heart raced like a galloping horse.

Aaron reached in his vest pocket and unfolded a paper. He walked over and handed it to Joseph's pa. His pa shook his head and frowned as he silently read.

"Here. Gimme that." Jeb snatched it out of his hand. "You all need to hear this." He read out loud. Aaron looked over his shoulder.

$150 Reward!
Moses
Ran away August 22
from Oakley plantation near Frederick, Maryland
Approximately twelve years old.
Tall for his age, about 5' 6"
Light of color, wearing a tow linen shirt and tan pants.
May be accompanied by a runaway woman
about age fifteen named Tillie.
$300 reward if this Negro is apprehended out-of-state.

Jeb stared at me with them demon eyes. He held up the wanted poster. "You gonna fetch me and Aaron here three hundred dollars." He puckered his lips at Tillie. "And a looker like you is worth a pretty penny."

I gritted my teeth. I wanted to jump off that seat and wrestle him to the ground. But that would spoil the plan.

I looped the reins through my fingers the way George taught me. Didn't pull up on them. Let them go slack. Joseph saw the reins in my hand. He walked between the horse and Aaron. "Maybe we should check with the sheriff on this one, Pa." He tilted his head toward me and Tillie.

Mr. Post stared at me. His eyes widened. He nodded and turned to Joseph. "Maybe you're right." He walked between the buggy and Jeb.

Joseph took off his hat and ran a finger inside the rim. "Maybe we should go to the house and talk about this."

Jeb put his gun in the holster. "Now you're talkin'."

Joseph spun around and smacked the horse's hindquarters with his hat. "Haw, Shadow! Haw! Give her her head, Moses!"

I snapped the reins hard. She dug down with her back legs and took off like a deer.

Joseph yelled, "Let Shadow take you—"

A shot fired. The bullet hit the ground next to the buggy wheel, spraying me and Tillie with dirt. Shadow took off at a dead run. I blinked dust out of my eyes. Tried to hang onto the reins and the seat at the same time. Tillie screamed. She fell to her knees. Threw her shawl over her head. Crouched under the seat.

Jeb cussed. "I'm gettin' the law after you!" More hollering. Grunting. Scuffling. Another shot fired. Somebody screamed. The voices died away like somebody threw a pail of water on a fire.

Shadow's hooves beat loud against the dirt road. The buggy wheels bounced over rocks and ruts.

Somebody yelled, "He's dead!"

I almost pulled up on the reins.

"Maybe we should go back," I shouted to Tillie.

She poked her head out from under the seat. She stared at me with them big eyes and laid a hand on my knee. "No, Mose. Keep goin'. I'm sure that was Jacob talkin'. Maybe he shot one of them snakes." She looked behind us. "Cain't see nothin'. Too dark. We's gettin' too far away. More lanterns is comin' by the house. Folks is turnin' out to see the ruckus." She looked up at me. "But none of them lanterns is comin' this way."

"Yeah, but they's bound to come after us soon. We gonna get blamed for that killin'. If we hadn't run away, nobody woulda got shot." My hands sweated so bad I thought the reins might slip out of my fingers. I knowed we shoulda gone back. It was gonna be worse for us now than if we turned ourselves in right away. Would they kill me, too? They had worse plans for Tillie. We had to keep running.

I wondered how long Shadow could gallop at full speed. She was bigger than any buggy horse I ever saw. Seemed liked she could haul a heavy load. I couldn't see too good in the lamplight, but she didn't look sweated up yet.

I took a peek at the sky. The stars were hiding. Must be a cloudy night. I hoped Shadow knew Star. But where was Shadow taking us?

Chapter 34
Toll Road

Even though the reins was slack and Shadow had her way, I been squeezing the leather so tight between my fingers they was getting numb. I loosened my thumb a bit. Dirt road and darkness stood before us. Trees like black ghosts rose up on either side.

Tillie hung onto the edge of her seat with both hands like the bench might fly away with her any time now. "How long can she run at full gallop? We've gone a mile or two. And where in heaven are we goin', Mose?"

"Dunno. But I sure hope we ain't going to heaven. We come too far to get trampled by a horse."

She started to sob but covered her mouth with her shawl and quieted herself right quick. Tears ran down my face, too. I hoped Tillie couldn't see them.

I hadn't dared to look back since we heard the killing. Hadn't heard no noise behind us. I nudged Tillie. "Could you look if anybody's following us?"

She grabbed the bench with one hand and the buggy cover with the other. She turned around. "My land. Oh, God in heaven."

"They after us?"

"No," she sobbed. "That's just it. They ain't. There ain't a light in sight. And I cain't hear nothin', neither."

I felt like somebody lifted a fifty-pound sack off my back. I straightened up and took a deep breath. "We gotta take a chance and ease up on Shadow, or we ain't gonna have a horse to take us no place." I pulled up gently on the reins. "Whoa, girl." We slowed to a trot. As Shadow settled into her new pace my heart settled down too. My neck and shoulders felt like they been playing tug of war. I stretched them out some. Tillie fiddled with her cap and shawl and smoothed out her skirt.

I looked up past the ghost trees to see if the stars came out. Sure enough, Star hung in the sky like a lantern.

We had gone a far piece when Shadow slowed to a walk then stopped. A long pole stretched across the road like a gate. Shadow turned to the edge of the road and dipped her nose in a water trough. I handed Tillie the reins and hopped off. I held Shadow's bridle and patted her head. "Easy, girl." I knew she could get sick if she drank too fast after working so hard.

"Mose," Tillie said, "is this where Shadow's takin' us?" She pointed to a building past the trough. "That house ain't no bigger than a slave shack.... I thought there wasn't no slaves up north."

My neck went stiff again. I ain't seen such a small house since I left the plantation. Did we come this far just to be slaves for somebody up north? Not everybody up here wanted to help runaways. I gripped Shadow's bridle tighter.

A man with a lantern opened the door. "Who goes there?"

Tillie whispered. "Let's go, Mose."

I held my breath. I couldn't think of nothing to say. "Come on, Shadow," I said. Maybe I could push open that gate and get her back on the road.

"The man swung the light toward us. "This is a toll road. You gotta pay the toll."

"Y-Yessir. Of course, sir." I turned to Tillie. "Hand me my tote." I still had the five dollars the abolitionist man gave me in Elmira.

"How much, sir?" Tillie asked. Her voice didn't shake—but her hand did. She held out two bits.

He took the money. "That'll do." He dropped it in his pocket and opened the gate.   My heart was at full gallop and it was gonna take a few minutes to slow it down. I climbed back on the seat. Tillie handed me the reins. Shadow walked through the gate like she'd done it before.

The man tipped his hat. "Hope you folks ain't got much farther to go this time of night."

Tillie smiled. "Thank you, sir." She watched him walk away. "Well, he went back in that little house." She turned to me and whispered, "That was close. I thought for sure that was Jeb comin' out that door. He even looked like him."

"Well, he didn't have no broken tooth." I didn't tell her I thought that man looked like Jeb too. Shadow trotted down the road like she knew her way. But she belonged to the Posts, and she was far from home.

I looked up in the sky. Star rode along next to us. I thought maybe we was headed west. But I knew Canada was north. I hoped our luck hadn't run out.

Chapter 35
Stagecoach Inn

It was morning when houses and buildings snuck up on us. Sun wasn't up yet, but light poked up from behind the mountains. I was glad everybody was asleep. Didn't know if this town was friendly. Didn't know if Shadow would stop here.

She made a sharp right turn down a road on the edge of town and trotted faster.

Tillie nudged me. "We almost there, ain't we?"

I nodded and swallowed hard.

Shadow jogged past an inn with a sign hanging out front and four stagecoaches parked next to it. She ran right into an open barn and stopped sudden-like. I put my arm out to keep Tillie from tumbling forward. I near fell off the bench myself.

A black boy stood in front of us holding a shovel full of horse manure. His mouth fell open wide enough to catch a horsefly. He tossed the brown mound into a cart and the shovel in after it. "Why Lordy, Lordy, it's Shadow." He laid hold of her bridle and petted her nose. A smile stretched across his face. He reached into his pocket, pulled out a small apple, and held it in the flat of his hand. Shadow scooped it with her big lips. "Wait till I tell Mr. Fanning you come home." The boy's big brown eyes looked up and down the buggy. "So how you like bein' a rich man's horse? Not enough to stay there, I reckon. I guess you'd rather pull a stagecoach." He finally looked at me and Tillie. "And Shadow, who this you drug home with you?"

He strolled over, wiped his hands on his pants, and shook my hand. "Hey, my name's Charlie. What's yours?"

He was shorter than me. His handshake felt strong for a boy. His eyes looked honest. I suspected he wasn't no slave. But what if he worked for Jeb or Aaron? Or somebody they was in cahoots with? I smiled anyway. "I'm Moses, and this here is Tillie."

He grinned then nodded toward the barn door. "Welcome to T.W. Fanning Stagecoach Company of Lockport, New York." He picked up a pitchfork and tossed hay into a stall. "You folks ridin' the mornin' stage?"

Tillie looked at me with them tin plate eyes. She rolled the edge of her shawl between her fingers and stared at Charlie.

I rubbed the leather reins between my fingers. Why didn't he ask us what we was doing here? It's not every day a runaway horse shows up in your barn with a couple of strangers. I looked up in the hayloft. Eyed every corner and stall. Nobody else was here.

I stepped out of the buggy and handed Charlie the reins. "Here, Charlie. Glad you and Shadow is friends. Sorry she ran away. Tillie and I will be goin'."

I reached up in the carriage and helped Tillie down. We turned away from Charlie and walked toward the door. I prayed he wouldn't stop us. I could almost feel that pitchfork in my back.

"Wait."

We stopped. I bit my lip. Looked at Tillie. We turned around.

He pointed the pitchfork with one hand. "You must be runaways."

I grabbed Tillie's hand and took a step backwards.

Charlie waved the pitchfork. "I mean—I know how you got here."

We walked back some more. About five steps and we would be out the door.

He looked at the pitchfork. "Oh, this." He threw it in the hay and held out his hands. "Don't worry. Nobody's gonna hurt you."

I swallowed hard. We stood still.

"The man who bought Shadow is friends with Mr. Fanning. Mr. Fanning's an abolitionist, too."

I let go of Tillie's hand. My heart slowed a bit.

He walked past us and waved us through the barn door. "You got to come meet him. He'll help you get to the border."

I grabbed his arm and stopped him. "Border? What border?"

He grinned. "The Canadian border."

I let go his arm. We kept walking. We passed by the stagecoaches. "The stage goes to Niagara," he said. "You'll be there by noon." He stepped in a doorway. "This is Washington House. Come on in." He disappeared inside.

I stood in front of the door, stuck to the ground like a rail post.

Tillie grabbed my hands. Tears ran down her dusty face. "Is it true? Is it true? It can't be. It can't be."

"Hush up. Somebody might hear you." I whispered. "I don't know. I hope it ain't some trick."

A red-haired man with a wide mustache stepped out from the inn. Charlie came out behind him. The man put his freckled hand on my shoulder and smiled. "Welcome, son. You must be Moses. T.W. Fanning, here. And I guess you're Tillie." He tipped his hat to her then put an arm around both of us and walked us to the barn. "We got some planning to do. It'll be safer there." Charlie followed us.

Mr. Fanning shut the barn door behind us.

A tall black man stood in the middle of the barn, removing Shadow's tack and traces. "Mornin', Mr. Fanning," he said without looking up.

"Morning, Dan." Mr. Fanning put a hand on my shoulder. "Don't worry. Dan works for me. He's a friend."

I blinked. How come I didn't see him in the barn before? Did he sneak in after we walked out? He reminded me of Aaron. I shook my head. I thought, *Get a hold of yourself, Mose. Every stranger ain't a traitor.*

Mr. Fanning patted Shadow on the nose as she munched hay. "Good to see you, girl." He turned to Dan. "Go ahead and put her in a stall. It'll be a few days before we can get her and this buggy back to the Posts. He turned to Charlie and put a finger to his lips. "And not a word about Moses and Tillie."

Charlie nodded. "You mean, sir…?"

He folded his arms. "Yes. Those men at the tavern are riding the morning stage." He frowned. "We don't know where their sympathies lie."

While Dan unhitched Shadow, Mr. Fanning sat down on a milk stool. He pointed to a pile of hay. "Please sit down." He leaned forward. "Did anyone follow you?"

We shook our heads. Tillie rolled the edge of her shawl in her fingers. "If anybody did, we couldn't see 'em."

He nodded. "That's good. Could there be anyone who knows you're here?"

Tillie spoke. "I ain't sure…."

"What about the Posts? Do they know you took off in the buggy?"

I bit my lip. Mr. Fanning's blue eyes looked kind—not mad, like we stole somebody's carriage. "Well, sir…they probably know. Joseph handed me the reins. Said Shadow would take us somewhere. I reckon he knowed she'd come here." I took a deep breath. If this man was a friend of the Posts, he needed to know everything.

I spit out the words. "That is…if they's alive."

Mr. Fanning closed his eyes and pinched his eyebrows together. "Tell me what happened."

Tillie sat and rocked back and forth, shaking her head. I looked back at Mr. Fanning. Still didn't see no anger in them eyes.

"Speak up, son."

"Well, sir…Joseph was taking us in the buggy to his place when some slave catchers stopped us…."

"Go on."

Joseph and his pa fought 'em off while we rode away."

He wrinkled his forehead. "What kind of fight?"

"A gunfight…sir. It was dark, and they was behind us. We heard a shot. Somebody said, 'He's dead.' It sounded like Joseph Post's voice…." I blinked back tears and looked at my shoes. "But we don't know who."

He stroked his chin. "So did he say it matter of fact. Just like that?"

"Yessir," I said.

"If the dead man was Joseph's pa I think Joseph would have sounded upset."

Tillie spoke up. "No, sir. He sounded surprised." She twisted the hem of her skirt around her finger. "Oh Mr. Fanning, I hope you is right. This man, Jeb, has been chasing us since we left Pennsylvania. And now a black man name of Aaron is helpin' him."

Dan stopped forking hay into the stall and looked over at Tillie.

Mr. Fanning stood up. "Something wrong, Dan?"

He frowned. "No, sir. It's just a shame, sir. That's all." He started pitching hay again. "Y'all come by way of Rochester?"

"Yessir," I said.

Mr. Fanning started pacing back and forth. "We have to get you two on the stage before Jeb and Aaron find you. Maybe one of them is dead. But maybe not. We can't take that chance."

I raised my eyebrows. "Pardon me, sir…but ain't them men over at the tavern riding that stage?"

He sat back down on the milk stool. "Well, let me think about this." He closed his eyes. "We carry mostly mail on the morning run. How about you ride on top with the mail bags."

Tillie said, "But everybody'll see us up there, for sure."

Mr. Fanning walked over to a corner of the barn and picked up a couple of empty grain sacks. "Come here, Moses." He held a sack up next to me. "Well, you're too big to fit inside one." He picked up another sack and stuck it over my head. "But if we put one over your head and shoulders, one on your feet, and split a sack or two to go around your middle, I think we can do it." He turned to Charlie. "Could you find me four more sacks?"

"Will do, Mr. Fanning." Charlie started searching the barn.

Mr. Fanning took a look out the barn door. "Phil is hitching the team now. Dan, you want to go help him?"

"Yes sir." He threw the pitchfork in the hay and walked out of the barn.

It wasn't long before Dan came running back. He caught his breath. "Pardon me, Mr. Fanning, but maybe these two shouldn't be takin' the stage."

"Why?"

"Those men in the tavern was talkin' about slavin' business."

"The two men riding this morning?"

"Yes, sir."

Mr. Fanning shook his head. "What were they saying?"

"One of 'em has a brother who's a bounty hunter. He's lookin' for a couple of runaways."

"Around Lockport?"

"Yes, sir."

"All the more reason we need to get them out of here."

Dan poked at some hay with his boot. "I could make them comfortable in one of them back stalls here in the barn where nobody can see 'em. Get them vittles. They'd be a lot stronger for the trip tomorrow with full bellies."

Mr. Fanning sighed. "Maybe you're right." He looked at us with troubled eyes and forced a smile. "We will get you two on that stage tomorrow. In the meantime, Dan will see to your needs." He turned toward the door. "Got to check on those passengers. Don't want them coming here looking for me." He patted Dan on the shoulder. "Thanks for your help." He walked out of the barn.

Dan smiled, put an arm around us both, and walked us to the back of the barn. "I gotta fine stall back here that'll make a good hidin' place." He forked a load of straw into the stall—enough for us to hide under if we needed to.

He fed and watered Shadow then took another horse out of the barn. I figured he had to hitch her to the stagecoach.

I pushed some straw into a mound and laid down. It wasn't no tick, but it'd do.

Tillie gave me the eye. She plopped herself down but sat against the back of the stall keeping a lookout for folks coming in the barn. "I wish we was goin' to Canada today." She twisted a piece of straw around her finger.

"I do too. But I guess we gotta wait."

I woulda made plans to hightail it on foot if it wasn't for the slavers being under our noses. Lord knows I didn't want to ride on top of that stagecoach. I made myself smile. "Look at it this way, Tillie. We didn't get no sleep last night. Now we can rest up for the trip tomorrow."

She fluffed up some straw and laid down. "I guess so, Mose, but somethin' doesn't feel right."

"Well, maybe you're just thinkin' about them slave catchers breathin' down our necks." I knowed I was fretting about it. I tried to put it out of my mind. I needed to sleep. I prayed the angels would hide us.

I woke up when somebody ran into the barn yelling, "Dan! Dan!"

Mr. Fanning ran up to us. "Either one of you see him?"

I sat up and rubbed my eyes. "No, sir. Not since he forked straw in the stall for us. He fed Shadow and took out that chestnut mare."

Mr. Fanning slapped his hat on his leg. "That's not like him to up and leave like that!" He shook his head. "The chestnut mare? That's his horse. Why would he run off when there's work to do? Where'd he go?"

"Don't know, sir." I looked at Tillie. She stared at me with them big brown eyes.

A short barrel-shaped man walked into the barn. He wiped dust off his face with his bandanna. "Back from Niagara. The weather held out for us."

"Glad to hear that," Mr. Fanning said. "Phil, meet Moses and Tillie." He turned to us. "This is Phil, our stagecoach driver." He looked back at Phil. "By any chance did you see where Dan went before you left this morning?"

"He rode down the turnpike toward Rochester. I thought it seemed kind of strange. When I asked him where he was headed, he said he was running errands for you."

Mr. Fanning shook his head. "I never told him any such thing." He folded his arms. "Isn't he from Rochester?"

Phil nodded. "Yeah. His brother, Aaron, lives there."

Mr. Fanning's eyes grew wide. "Aaron!"

A chill ran down my back like a cold hand.

Tillie let out a cry and clapped a hand over her mouth.

Mr. Fanning slapped his hat on his leg. "That changes everything."

Phil frowned. "I don't get it."

Mr. Fanning sat on a milk stool and folded his hands. He looked up at Phil. "Moses and Tillie were supposed to take the stage today. We were gonna hide them with the mailbags."

Phil nodded. "Oh yeah. Charlie said we had *extra freight* to load on top, but said it would have to wait till tomorrow."

"Yes. The plan is to hide these two with the mail sacks." He closed his eyes and shook his head. "I just hope Dan and his brother don't come back here searching for them."

Phil looked over at us then back at Mr. Fanning. "What do you mean?"

Just as Mr. Fanning started to talk, Tillie jumped to her feet. "He mean that Dan's brother, Aaron, is a slave catcher. And Dan heard us tellin' Mr. Fanning 'bout the two slavers, Aaron and Jeb, who almost grabbed us in Rochester. They got into a gunfight with the Posts. Somebody got killed. Mighta been Dan's brother." She looked at me with fire in her eyes. "Why that cockroach. I bet he lied 'bout slavers ridin' the stage and lookin' for us. Pretendin' to help us out when all he wanted was to buy time so he could catch us before we got to the border."

"But we cain't know for sure, Tillie," I said.

Phil held up his hands. "Wait a minute. Tillie is right. Those passengers yesterday weren't slavers. They told me how upset they were about the new law. They've hidden a few slaves themselves and wondered if it was worth the risk anymore."

Tillie stared at me. "And what you have to say 'bout that, Moses?"

I swallowed hard. Stood up. My hands was sweating. I wiped them on my pants. "I think Tillie and I best be goin', Mr. Fanning. Don't want to cause you folks no more trouble. If we leave now, maybe we can get to Canada before them slave catchers get back." I took Tillie's hand and we started to walk out.

Mr. Fanning rose up off that milk stool and laid a firm hand on my shoulder. "Now wait a minute, son. We need to think this through. I know it's likely he's coming back for you. But it would be a whole lot safer for you to ride the stage tomorrow morning. If you leave now someone might see you and turn you in. And I don't recommend traveling on foot at night. You might be greeted by a pack of wolves. Besides, there's a mean-looking river you have to cross to get to Canada."

Me and Tillie stared at each other. I didn't like the idea of fighting more wolves. Maybe we wouldn't be so lucky this time.

Phil pulled a pistol out of a black holster that hung around his middle. "I always carry this for protection. And I have a rifle on the stage. You'd be safer with me. I can take you right to the bridge that'll take you over that wild river."

Mr. Fanning nodded. "And a free black couple are riding the stage tomorrow to visit relatives in Canada. No worries there. Please think about it. We're here to help you."

"Okay," I said. "Could you give me and Tillie some time to talk it over?"

"Sure." Mr. Fanning patted my shoulder. He and Phil walked out of the barn.

Tillie wrung her hands. "How we know we can trust Phil? Maybe he just waitin' till we get outta town so's he can turn us in or blow our heads off."

I shook my head. "He ain't gonna do that. Mr. Fanning trusts him."

"Yeah, well Mr. Fanning trusted Dan too."

"But we gotta get to that bridge. Otherwise, we cain't get across. Phil can take us there."

"If Aaron and Dan don't get us first."

"You really want to face another pack of wolves by ourselves? I say we trust Phil."

Tillie slumped onto the straw and closed her eyes. "All right, Mose. All right. I pray the good Lord keep us safe from Aaron and Dan…and Jeb."

Another cold chill ran down my back. I couldn't let Jeb get Tillie. I sat down and put an arm around her shoulder. "Don't forget, my mama's prayin' too."

Chapter 36
Ride to Niagara

At dawn the next morning Charlie greeted us with hot cornbread and bacon. "I know it's early, but as soon as you finish breakfast we're gonna load you with the mailbags. Nobody's up yet snoopin' around."

Me and Tillie filled our bellies while we listened to Charlie jabber on about how we was almost there. He said plenty of other runaways rode the stage and made it. I didn't ask if there was anybody that got caught.

We walked outside.

The stagecoach stood a full head taller than a man. It had a round body with a door in the middle and windows with leather curtains. The driver's bench sat just below the railing that went around the flat top. Charlie loaded bags in a hold that stuck out the back while Phil checked the tack and traces on the three chestnut horses and one bay. He climbed up to the driver's seat easy as a wildcat climbing a mountain.

"Come on, Moses." He reached down with a black-gloved hand and pulled me up to the driver's bench. I crawled over the railing and flattened out. Tillie clambered over the railing and lay next to me. Charlie handed us up the burlap. I put one bag over my feet and wrapped the split one around my middle. Tillie did, too.

Phil stepped over the rail. "Send up the mail, Charlie." He stood over us as Charlie passed bags up. Phil stacked them high next to us. It felt a lot like lying in a wagon bed with sacks of corn piled around. All I could see now was his bearded face. "Got to cover up now. Want some help?"

"Thank you, sir, but I can do it." I helped Tillie pull the bag over her head and shoulders. Then I dragged the sack over my own head.

Burlap was a loose enough weave. We wouldn't have no trouble breathing. But it did make my nose itch.

Tillie reached for my hand. I snuck it from under the burlap and held her fingers.

"I'm scared," she whispered.

"Got good reason," I whispered back. I wondered if we shoulda run when we had the chance.

Footsteps headed our way. "Will you be coming back this way soon?" It was Mr. Fanning's voice.

A man answered. "We're purchasing lumber at the saw mill in Niagara. Plan to come back next week."

"Well, in that case, you'll want to take the train. Fastest way to get cargo from there to here," Mr. Fanning said. "An incredible invention, those steam engines. Maybe I should invest in them. Lord knows they're putting stagecoach companies out of business. I only make half the runs I used to. Have a safe trip."

"Thank you, sir."

The door shut. The stage wobbled a bit as they sat down in their seats. Phil barked a command. "Haw!" He snapped the reins. The stage jerked forward.

Mr. Fanning didn't say nothing about them black folks buying lumber. I wondered if slave catchers sat underneath us.

The stage bounced so much my head knocked against the floor. I scooted my head onto a mailbag.

We been on the road awhile when Tillie started to moan.

"Hush," I whispered. "Don't give us away."

"Mose…I gettin' sick. Cain't take this rockin'."

Besides bouncing up and down, the stage rocked back and forth. The mailbags kept shifting. Sometimes we did, too.

I whispered, "Lie on your side. Double up. Rest your head on a mailbag." I wished I could tell her to take the burlap off her head. I knowed I wanted to. Couldn't see a blamed thing. I felt woozy. Hoped we wouldn't throw up our breakfast all over them mailbags.

Seemed like we been up there all day when the stage stopped. Tillie took my hand and squeezed my fingers.

Phil climbed down and opened the stagecoach door. "Welcome to the village of Niagara, folks. Let me get your bags." He walked to the back and opened the hold.

"Want any help with them mail sacks?" a man asked.

"No thanks. The post office will send someone over. Go get yourselves some chow at the Cataract House. It's been a long ride."

Phil clucked at the horses and we road a bit farther.

We came to a stop.

Tillie whispered, "What's that noise, Mose? Ain't it strange?"

"Yeah." I couldn't rightly tell if it roared like a bear or hissed like a snake. Maybe it was a demon. Maybe it was Dan.

Phil climbed up over the railing. He whispered, "Glad we got you this far, but we can't take any chances. If Dan has a fast horse, he could be here anytime. Won't take him long to figure out you took the stage." He pulled the sacks off of our heads. I unwrapped myself and helped Tillie.

He took a bandanna out of his pocket and gently wiped sweat off of Tillie's face. "Listen. I brought you up to the suspension bridge. Just walk across and you'll be in Canada. He got down and gave Tillie a hand getting off. I jumped to the ground. I could see the bridge about a stone's throw away. Phil took Tillie's arm and we walked to the bridge.

A toll keeper met us.

"I'd like to pay for a couple of pedestrians," Phil said.

"Yes, sir. Fare is twenty-five cents a person."

Phil laid his hand on my shoulder and spoke to me gentle-like. "Don't be afraid. I've been over this bridge before. Even taken the stage across a time or two. Them thick cables are made of wire. So are the supporting cables attached to the bridge. They're made to hold a ton of weight." He patted my shoulder. "I'm headed for the post office, but I'll keep a look out for Dan. You've got to go. God be with you."

We stood in front of the bridge, stiff as Miz Oakley's china dolls.

As much as we been running about the country, we ain't never seen nothing like this. That giant bridge crossed the widest, maddest river we ever saw. Mr. Fanning said this was a mean river. Was it full of bears and snakes? I rubbed my hands together. They felt like ice.

Two wide black towers taller than hotels stood like giants in front of us. Two more giants guarded the other side of the river. Thick ropes stretched from the towers on one side of the river to the towers on the other. Smaller lines ran down from the big ropes and hooked to the wooden walkway. That bridge hung in the air like a clothesline between two trees. I didn't see how it could hold a body's weight. It only looked to be about ten paces wide—just wide enough for a buggy to get across. Seemed like a good wind could blow it right into that churning river.

I told my legs they was gonna have to walk across, even if they didn't like it. I kept thinking of Mama's words about Moses in the Bible. His mama said her child wasn't gonna be a slave no more. Well you know what, Mama? Your child ain't gonna be a slave, neither.

Chapter 37
Mad Water

I took Tillie's cold hand in mine, hoping I could warm hers up a little. We stepped onto the shiny wood planks. The bridge felt solid under my feet. Made me believe it could carry a stagecoach like Phil told us. But those boards was wet and slick.

The bridge stood high above the river. Two of them giant towers coulda been stacked in the river one on top of another, and still not reach us. Even so, the water roared louder and louder.

But the river wasn't no bear. It was a snake. The biggest, meanest snake I ever laid eyes on. It foamed and twisted and thrashed like its head was stuck in a trap. It spit spray all the way to the bridge. Upstream, more water gushed over a cliff into the river. If it wasn't for the chill in the air, I'd a thought we was crossing into hell. I had to remind myself— we wasn't going *to* hell; we was leaving it.

Tillie slid on the slippery wood. I catched her by the arm. She clung to me like a wet rag.

"Come on now. You can do it." I tried to smile. That blamed spray covered everything. Snake spit. That's what it was. Slimy snake spit.

We kept on, stepping more careful now, mindful of every plank in front of us. I looked over the side. My belly churned. I told myself I'd grab one of those cables if I slipped and fell.

Tillie squeezed my hand. "Look. We almost there, Mose. See the end of the bridge? We is halfway there."

She looked back. "How far you think we've.... She saw something that cut her words short. She dropped my hand and covered her mouth. Her eyes got wide. Wider than her tin plate eyes ever did. She was scared.

Two horsemen trotted toward us. I couldn't make out their faces under their broad-brimmed hats, but one man was white and one was black. I was betting the black man was Dan. Was the other man Jeb? The white man pointed at us and said something to his partner. They broke into a gallop.

Them hoof beats shook the planks. My heart about dropped into that river.

I grabbed Tillie's hand. "Come on."

She hiked up her skirt so she could run better. We took off down the middle of that bridge.

I didn't dare look back, but I could hear them hoof beats getting closer and closer. All the time that river snake hissed like it was rooting them on.

Tillie slid on the wooden planks. *Thud.*

I yanked her up, but her shoe got hooked in the hem of her skirt. I lost my grip on her. She fell again and slid toward the edge of the bridge.

Them hoof beats came up on us like thunder. The white man reined his horse, threw a noose around Tillie's middle, and dragged her up next to him. She gasped and cried and tried to pull at the rope, but he drew it tight around her elbows. She couldn't move her arms.

If Tillie's eyes woulda been bullets, he woulda been dead. "I ain't goin' with you, Jeb!"

The black man threw a rope at me, but I grabbed it and pulled it off my head before he could tighten it. I yanked the rope as hard as I could and tried to pull him off his horse. I took him unawares. He didn't count on me fighting back. He lost his balance and pulled on the reins to get himself upright. The horse reared and bolted forward. It lost its footing, slid on the slippery bridge, and fell on him, knocking him out cold.

I ran up next to that black traitor lying under his horse. A Judas—that's what he was. Maybe he was getting what he deserved. His hat had been knocked off and lay next to him. I took a good look at his face. It was Dan. I figured Aaron must be dead.

His horse struggled to get up and trotted back down the bridge.

I turned around to help Tillie. I grabbed the rope and tried to yank Jeb off his horse, but he was ready for me. He kicked me in the face. I fell backwards and slid near the edge of the bridge. I grabbed one of them support cables and held on. My head was spinning. I saw stars. I hung onto the cable with both hands and pulled myself up. My knees felt wobbly, but I could stand.

Jeb wrapped the rope tight around his arm. I figured he was making sure Tillie didn't go nowhere. He got off his horse. He pulled a pair of shackles out of his saddlebag.

I'd seen runaways put in irons before. Them things looked like a couple of bear traps. Hard and cold and mean.

"Hold out your hands," he growled. He shut the jaws of them things around Tillie's wrists and cackled like a hunter trussing up a deer.

Tillie looked up and saw me standing on the bridge, still holding onto the cable. Her eyes wasn't scared no more. I reckon she had given up. Like a fish on a hook that just quit fighting. Jeb seemed to think so, by the sneer on his face and the hungry look in his eye.

Jeb turned to me. "So, you comin' along with your perty sister?"

My belly twisted hearing them words. I looked over at Dan. Not moving. Maybe he was dead.

I set my eyes on Canada, just over the bridge. I was sure I could outrun Jeb. Easy. Besides, I didn't think he would give up his prize to come after me. Right then and there I coulda high-tailed it up the bridge, free as a white man. But Tillie's sad eyes woulda haunted me for the rest of my life. I couldn't leave her to face Jeb alone. If I couldn't set her free, then I was gonna go with her. I had my hunting knife. Might come in handy if there was a chance to get away.

I nodded my head.

He laughed at me like the devil himself.

I looked away. Didn't want to see those demon eyes.

I thought—forgive me, Mama. I ain't no Moses after all. I'm sorry I let you down. I just hope you understand. I cain't let Tillie go back alone.

Tillie half smiled at me. Some light came back in her eyes. I couldn't smile back.

Jeb reached in his bag and pulled out some more irons. He turned his back on Tillie. "Well, git over here," he told me.

I closed my eyes, took a step, and stuck out my hands.

I heard footsteps on the bridge. Opened my eyes. My heart stopped.

Tillie grabbed that rope, even with her hands shackled together, and pulled Jeb backwards. She took a running leap over the bridge with that rope around her middle. He fell over with her, the rope yanking his arm like a hangman's noose.

I ran to the edge and watched them fall into the mouth of the big river snake. All the way down, Jeb held onto them irons. The ones meant for me.

I fell on my knees and bawled harder than I ever did. Even when I had to leave Mama.

Chapter 38
Free

I looked out the schoolhouse window. Snow was falling. Funny how it could rush to the ground and make no noise. I blew on my fingers, trying to warm my hands. My new friends in Sandwich, Canada West, went on about how cold the winters was up here. Well, I wasn't complaining. I'd rather freeze in Canada than work them tobacco fields in Maryland.

I rubbed the bump on my nose. Jeb had broke it when he kicked me in the face. It didn't hurt no more. I opened up my Townsend Speller. I had to share it with Elijah who sat next to me, but I didn't mind. I learnt to spell near every word in this book. Our teacher, Miz Mary Gibb had forty-six students now. All of us black. All of us learning. All of us proud.

Miz Gibb always been free. And a Quaker. She got a good education in Boston and wanted to see other blacks learn to read and write. She and her husband, Henry, started a newspaper this month, *The Voice of the Fugitive*. First black newspaper in Canada. And it was started by a black man who used to be a slave.

It's been three months since I crossed into Canada. It's the Lord's doing how I came to get here. Who knows how long I mighta stayed on that bridge if the toll keeper hadn't run up to me. He throwed his arm around my shoulder, picked up my tote in his other hand, and walked me over into the Promised Land.

He took me to the Free Soil Hotel right there in Niagara. When I walked into that dark little building, the owner, Mr. Patterson, sat me down at a table next to the fire and tended to my nose. Then he ladled me a big bowl of hot soup. The toll keeper musta told him the goings on at the bridge because Mr. Patterson just smiled and let me be. Said if I needed anything to just ask. I nodded. I was so broke up over Tillie, I couldn't talk. I set that tote in my lap and twisted the cord around my finger. I been carrying that sack ever since Mama made it for me. I woulda been so sorry if I left behind the one thing I could remember her by. I wish I knowed that toll keeper's name so I could thank him.

My eyes was filling up with tears again when Henry Bibb walked through the door. He and Mr. Patterson was gabbing about what kind of business Henry was doing in town when Mr. Patterson whispered something to him. Henry looked my way. He walked over to me and sat down.

He laid his warm hand on my arm and smiled. Invited me to come home with him where his wife had a school. Said there was other runaways like me where he lived. I didn't say much, but nodded and smiled. Didn't want to start bawling like a baby in front of him. But I took him up on his offer.

So that's how I got to come to this school. Henry Bibb says someday I can be an abolitionist just like him, writing and telling people how bad slavery is. Ain't that just what Tillie used to tell me? How I miss her.

You ain't gonna die for nothing, Tillie. I'm gonna make you proud. Someday I'm gonna tell folks how you saved my life. I'm here today because of you.

I told Miz Mary Bibb about Mama. Miz Bibb say if I write my mama a letter, she'll print it in the paper. Maybe somebody will see it who knows my mama's whereabouts. They'd know where to find me. Miz Bibb even gave me a quill pen.

I took it out of my tote and rolled it in my fingers. It felt light and smooth and skinnier than a pencil. I thought about how Tillie and I wrote stuff and hid it in the sideboard in Miz Palmer's cellar. Them words was hid away where nobody could see. But lots of people in Canada and America might see my letter to Mama. I dipped the pen in the inkwell:

Dear Mama,

Your dream has come true. But it was a hard dream. I met many good folks along the way and some bad ones. There was times when I was lost and scared and times when I thought I'd be a slave again or dead. Whenever bad things happened, I remembered the things you taught me. The North Star led me to freedom. Your boy is free.

I'm living with Henry and Mary Bibb in Sandwich, Canada. I do chores for them. I get plenty to eat and I get to go to Miz Mary's school. I'm learning to read and write.

The Bibbs been so good to me, I could never repay them. But know, Mama, that what you done for me is worth much more. You kept telling me I was free from the day I was born. That gave me a heart to be free.

Just know, Mama, that you can be proud of me. I will try to be the man that you raised me to be. I don't know why there's so much evil in the world and why so many good people have to hurt, but you taught me that God has a plan for my life, and now I know that's true. I'm gonna write about slavery and be an abolitionist. I'm gonna help others get free, too.

I pray this letter finds you. I pray that God leads me to you. I want you to know, Mama, that I will never stop looking for you. I will never stop loving you. You had a dream for me. Now I have a dream for you. That we will be together again.

Your free son,
Moses